I0761918

VIOLET SKY
AVENGING LOVE

VIOLET SKY AVENGING LOVE

EVE MARIAN

Paige Publishing

January 2022 First Edition

ISBN-eBook: 978-1-7778013-8-0
ISBN-paperback: 978-1-7778013-9-7
ISBN-hardcover: 978-1-7780262-0-1

To anyone who has read a happily ever after,
and still wanted more.

One

Michaela

I panted and moaned. A bead of sweat dripped down my back as I sucked in a deep breath and held it, hoping it would help, but it was no use. It would not fit.

"Michaela, is everything all right?" Hunter called out. I exhaled loudly, releasing my stomach muscles, and let the gold sequined dress pool at my feet. I kicked it in frustration.

"I'm fine. I'll be a few more minutes though," I called back from our bedroom. Padding across the carpeted room, I searched for another dress to wear. None of my old clothes fit since having Violet. I really should have thought about buying something new. Tonight was the Academy's graduation dinner. As a lecturer at the school, I looked forward to seeing my students but dreaded finding something to wear. I'd put it off until the last minute and now I was stuck.

A knock at the bedroom door was all the warning I got before Hunter walked in.

"I'm not dressed yet," I said and covered my body with my hands.

He walked toward me, slowly raking his gaze over me. The heat from his eyes raised goosebumps on my flesh, but I still did not drop my hands.

I crossed both arms to cover my body and one leg over the other. He moved to stand in front of me and ran his middle finger along my arm, from my elbow up to my shoulder. He then cupped my face.

"What's wrong?" he whispered when my gaze remained focused on the floor.

Tears burned behind my eyes, but I squeezed them shut. A few treasonous drops escaped and humiliation threatened to drown me. *I would not cry over a dress.*

Hunter ran his fingers along my neck, back toward my face, until he stopped at my chin. He tipped it up and waited. When I finally opened my eyes, the intensity in his stare loosened my muscles and my arms fell limply to my sides.

"Tell me what's bothering you," he demanded in a low voice. His creased brow softened the command.

"My dress doesn't fit." I hoped the words didn't sound as petulant to him as they did to me.

He smiled and ran his other hand down my back until he cupped my backside. "I love your new curves," he growled in my ear.

I pushed him back and crossed my arms over my chest, this time in anger. "I'm serious, Hunter. This dress doesn't fit, and neither does anything else in my closet. I don't know what I'm going to do. I wanted to go shopping this week, but Violet wouldn't settle and I had course prep to do, and dress shopping was the last thing I thought about. Until now."

Hunter stopped caressing my arms when I finished my rant. Rubbing his chin, he assessed my stance, then strode inside my walk-in closet. He turned on the light and looked around until he spotted something. He pulled out a blue wrap dress I had worn the first time we kissed.

"Try this on." He passed me the dress, which still hung on the hanger. My lips turned up in annoyance and I may have pouted a little. *This dress could work.* The wrap would be more forgiving around my curves and I wouldn't have to fight a zipper to get it on.

"All right, give me two minutes, then we can go." I snatched the dress from his hand, then turned and rose on my toes. Steadying myself with a hand on his shoulder, I kissed him gently on the cheek. "Thank you," I said and smiled.

His eyes crinkled, and he pulled me closer. "You missed." His mouth moved gently on my lips, and I sighed in response. "I'll meet you outside in five minutes."

I nodded and shooed him out.

Ten minutes later, wrapped snugly in my blue dress and three-inch heels, I stepped out and watched for Hunter's response. Distracted by his phone, he didn't notice when I walked up behind him, seated at the kitchen table. I tried to peer over his shoulder at his screen, but he turned it over quickly and shoved the phone in his pocket. He stood from the table and smiled at me. I frowned.

"What were you reading?" I asked.

"Nothing. Just some news in Norway."

I tilted my head but narrowed my eyes. "The news?"

"Yes," he said, lifting his head. His lips curled up when he noticed my dress. "You look beautiful."

I couldn't help but smile back. His happiness was contagious to me. He stood and stuck out his elbow and tilted his head while he waited for me to grab hold. Raking my gaze over his navy-blue suit and amber tie, the color matching his eyes perfectly; my chest tightened. He took my breath away every time he looked at me like that.

"Yeah, I'm ready," I sighed and grabbed my purse before leaving our penthouse. "Do you think Violet will be okay with my grandmother?"

"Of course," he said while holding the elevator door. "She raised two kids of her own. She cares for her as much as we do."

"I guess you're right." I checked my phone anyway to make sure I didn't have any unread messages from her.

Nothing.

I let out another sigh and tried to put my worries aside for tonight.

***

Hunter drove up to the front entrance of the hotel, where a valet waited for us. After handing over the keys, he came around to open the car door for me. I reached for his outstretched hand and stepped out of the car. The night was chillier than I had expected for May, but fortunately, the hotel lobby was only a few steps away. Once inside, we followed the signs directing us to the graduation reception.

"Geez, any graduation ceremony I've ever had was in a school gymnasium or on campus. I've never seen anything like this before," I told Hunter.

They held the party in a private room, which reminded me of a ballroom from a regency romance novel. Couples danced on the parquet floor in the center while rows of people stood by and watched or chatted among each other. Low-hanging crystal chandeliers and red velour drapes hung throughout the room.

He shrugged. "Manticores tend to have a flair for the dramatic."

I snorted indelicately. I would describe everything that happened in the last year of my life as quite dramatic.

"Well, if it isn't the lovely and magnificent Michaela with her bore of a husband," a voice rumbled behind me. I turned and landed face to face with Hunter's cousin, Leo. Hunter groaned beside me, but a grin spread across my face.

"Well, if it isn't the devilishly charming, Leo," I countered.

"Guilty as charged." He gave a slight bow in acknowledgment, then extended his hand. I placed my palm on top of his. As usual, he curled his fingers, leaned forward, and kissed my hand instead of shaking it.

"Leo, what brings you out of your shallow hole?" Hunter asked.

"Professor Wallace asked me to come, and I would have refused if the delectable Vivienne hadn't looked so eager to have me join the graduation reception," he crooned.

"Vivienne?" I asked. "Who's she?"

For a moment, Leo's smiling face froze. His eyes widened, but he recovered quickly and his smooth smile returned. "Vivienne is an old acquaintance of Hunter's," he said. "She was in France for a bit and recently returned."

Hunter didn't offer any further explanation.

Of course, Hunter had a past before me, several decades' worth, and I certainly dated other people before I met him. This information did not exactly surprise me. But Leo's reaction alerted my jealous instincts.

"Where is the—what did you call her—delectable Vivienne?" I asked, a little too sweetly.

"She's the one coming straight for us," Leo muttered and covered his mouth with his drink.

A tall, lithe supermodel walked toward us. My jaw dropped and my eyes bugged out. I was certain I looked like some cartoon character. *That was Hunter's ex-girlfriend?* Oh, for goodness sakes, really? Her smooth satin dress hugged her body. Nothing jiggled or moved. It all just stayed where she wanted it to. I was sure she hadn't fallen over in her bedroom earlier trying to squeeze into her dress, either. I pasted a smile on my face and straightened my spine, hoping to look a little taller than my five-foot-four frame.

She smiled back, but her eyes remained large and doll-like. They didn't retract into half-moons as mine did. Her pouty lips were naturally full and her long fingers perfectly polished.

"You must be Michaela," she said with a sultry voice and lifted her hand to me. *Oh, for the love of all that is holy, she had a sexy voice too!* I shook her long and slender hand and may have squeezed a little too hard. She either didn't let on or my weak attempt to intimidate her was no match for this Amazon woman.

"Hunter, it's wonderful to see you again," she said, while her gaze roamed over his body. "You look great."

I was too busy staring at *Wonder Woman* to notice Hunter's reaction, but his voice remained cool and unbothered. "Thank you, Vivienne. I'm sorry you could not make it to the wedding, but I'm glad you can finally meet my wife, Michaela." Hunter tucked his arm around my waist and pulled me closer to him. I did a little happy dance in my head.

Vivienne smiled, but it did not soften her face—it was still perfectly smooth, no crease or wrinkle in sight. "I've heard a lot about you, Michaela," she said.

"All good, I hope," I answered back and laughed. Her lips twitched. I waited a few more heartbeats for a response, but she only addressed Hunter with her next words. "I was hoping I could speak to you, privately."

I raised my eyebrows, but neither Hunter nor Vivienne noticed.

"Whatever you have to say, you can say it in front of Michaela," Hunter responded. I smirked and refrained from folding my arms beneath my chest. It wasn't easy.

"From what I've heard, Michaela can take care of herself in a room full of manticores," said Vivienne, her eyes scanning me, looking for any hints at the stories she must have heard. I thought her eyes narrowed when she looked into mine, but I couldn't be sure. "Besides, it is not my request, but Professor Wallace's. And your father's."

Hunter's father, King Marsel Durand, ruled over all manticores. He and I got off on the wrong foot, but we'd become remarkably close after we both aired our grievances, and especially since Violet came along. It surprised me to hear he wanted to speak to Hunter alone. But I didn't want to seem insecure or put Hunter in an awkward position to defend me against his king's direct request, so I said, "It's no problem. I was planning to catch up with some of the students, anyway."

Hunter squeezed my hand and a small exhale escaped from his

lips. He leaned down next to my ear and whispered, "I'll be back in just a few minutes."

"Don't hurry back, I've got Leo to keep me company," I said with a smirk. Because really, I wasn't all that selfless. I enjoyed needling Hunter.

For his part, Leo offered a wide grin and waggled his eyebrows. I couldn't help but laugh.

"Let's go and let's make this quick," Hunter said to Vivienne.

"Well played," said Leo as we watched Hunter and Vivienne walk out of the room together. I wasn't feeling so sure about my decision anymore. I frowned at how beautiful they looked together. "How close were the two of them?"

"They were pretty close," said Leo, raising his eyebrow. Perhaps realizing his words were not comforting, he added, "But Hunter was the one who broke things off. I wouldn't worry about Vivienne."

"Mmm, right," I said, then wanting to change the subject, I asked him, "What do you think the king wants to talk to Hunter about, anyway?"

"I don't know, but I need to speak to the king as well."

"What about?"

"Something I read in the news today. Something about a mauling in Norway that sounds a bit too much like a manticore attack."

"Is it something we should be concerned about?"

"When it comes to manticore attacks, we must always be concerned if one makes the news."

"Even though it happened so far away?"

"Distance doesn't keep us safe. Not for long anyway."

I frowned and wondered if this was the reason the king wanted to speak with Hunter. If so, why would he keep it from me?

"I don't think it's anything to worry about yet. Come, let's get a drink."

I took Leo's arm and walked with him toward the bar. "Are you sure I don't need to worry about Vivienne?" The image of the beautiful woman still etched in my mind.

Leo knocked the rest of his drink back and stared at the door Vivienne and Hunter had exited through a few minutes ago. "Michaela, sweetheart, Vivienne is the least of your troubles right now."

"She is?" But just as the words left my mouth, I spotted Laura, Hunter's sister, rushing toward me with a microphone in her hand.

"Laura's going to ask you to make a speech, I'm sure of it, and no one can say no to Laura."

I groaned because Laura had a way of making everyone do her bidding, and I was no exception. I could stand up to a manticore threatening to kill me, but I hadn't found the nerve to stand up to her. *Maybe tonight would be the night?*

"Michaela, darling, could you say a few words to the graduating class? It would mean so much to them to hear you speak, both as their lecturer and as a member of the royal family. I'm sure you wouldn't want to disappoint them." Her face beamed at me and I could have sworn she winked, too.

"Of course not," I said and exhaled the breath I held. Nope, tonight would not be the night.

Two

Hunter

I hadn't seen Vivienne in years. We had crossed paths on several occasions, but this was the first time we were alone together. I followed her into the elevator. Standing shoulder to shoulder, I felt her stare but kept my gaze on the mirrored doors. I had nothing to say and was uninterested in small talk. Unfortunately, Vivienne must have felt differently.

"How have you been?" she asked.

"Great. Really good," I said and slid my hands into my pant pockets. She continued to stare.

"We never discussed things after the last time we argued," she began but I cut her off.

"There's nothing more to say, Vivienne. We've been over it a hundred times already."

From the corner of my eyes, I saw her run her hand through her long, straight black hair and puff out a sigh. "Well, maybe you said all you wanted to say, but I didn't."

"Vivienne—"

"I just want to say, I'm sorry."

Her apology caught me off-guard. Vivienne had never apologized. She had rationalized, ostracized, and even antagonized me, but this was the first apology I'd heard from her lips. I turned to face her. Her eyes did not shy away from my hard stare, but they softened. Her lips pouted a bit, then she smiled. "I know I don't say it very often."

"You have never said it, actually."

She pouted again, but then smoothed out a smile. "I'm a proud woman, I'll admit it. But I have also learned to admit when I am wrong."

I nodded but said nothing.

"So?" she crooned.

"What do you want from me, Vivienne?" I had turned back to face the elevator doors and was saved from her response when they opened. I walked out, but Vivienne pulled me back and held me in place with both hands on my upper arms.

"I am asking for your forgiveness, Hunter." Her fingers tightened.

I sighed and shook my head.

"I know it's over now that you're with Michaela, but I don't want to think you still hate me."

I laughed out loud at this, but it held no mirth. "You lost me when you did what you did, Vivienne. It was over way before Michaela."

And when she waited for me to say more, I added, "And I don't hate you. I never did."

You must love someone to hate them. The opposite of love isn't hate, it's indifference.

"So, where is my father?" I asked, looking around.

"I am here," said a familiar voice behind me. I turned, but Vivienne's fingers were still clutching my sleeve. My father's eyes narrowed when he saw Vivienne's grip on my arm and he frowned. *Great.*

I gently pried her manicured fingers away and walked toward the ruler of the Manticore Kingdom, who also happened to be a very displeased father right now.

"What's going on?" I asked, hoping to avoid any mention of Vivienne's hands on my body.

Glaring at Vivienne, he said, "I asked Professor Wallace to bring you to the basement because I needed to discuss something and I didn't want any manticores within earshot," he explained. "However, I did not expect to find you here with her."

"Professor Wallace was busy with the graduates and needed someone to escort Hunter to the basement. I volunteered," she explained.

"I'm sure you did," said the king. His voice did not sound grateful.

Stoically, Vivienne kept her gaze steady and did not look down.

"Why did you need to speak to me privately?" I asked my father.

He turned to Vivienne. "Thank you for bringing Hunter downstairs. If you'll excuse us now."

"Yes, of course." She gave one last glance in my direction, then walked away. My father waited until she turned the corner before he continued.

"Have you seen the news?"

I didn't have to ask which news story he referred to. "Yes, I did."

"You must fly to Norway tomorrow, find out if there's anything we need to take care of immediately."

"Norway? Tomorrow? Isn't that a bit soon? There's only been one attack. Let's give the magistrate in Norway a chance to take care of this on her own before we swoop in. It could look like we don't think they can handle their own affairs."

My father pursed his lips. "Two attacks and I've already spoken with Astrid. She's the one who asked us to come. Our aid does not threaten her, in fact, she is wise enough to request it."

"Two? But I have heard nothing about the other one yet."

"It just happened tonight. Astrid said she got there before the media did, but they were lucky this time. She doesn't want to risk another attack and another story getting out."

A second attack, only one day later. Astrid was right to be concerned. Someone was looking for attention and now they had it. "All right, I'll leave first thing in the morning for Norway. I'll just tell Michaela it is for manticore business."

"You will not be bringing Michaela with you?" My father leaned back and crossed his arms over his chest. "I think she could be a real asset to you. She was the one responsible for saving the kingdom in the last three coup attempts. Why not bring her?"

"Because she is not the kingdom's weapon. She's my wife and Violet's mother. I do not want to bring her into the line of fire."

"If you do not bring her, I suspect you will be in the line of fire with her wrath. She does not seem the type to be placated easily."

"No, that's why she can't know the truth."

"It is never a good idea to lie to a woman, son. No good comes from it."

"Thank you for your advice, but I'm going to take my chances."

"Then I wish you luck on your mission and your marriage."

My father's sardonic smile made me hesitate. For a moment, I thought about telling Michaela the truth, but I quickly dismissed it. No—keeping her safe would be the best thing I could do for my wife. If she ever found out, she would understand my decision, of course.

"If that is all, I will head back upstairs and join Michaela. I've already been gone too long."

"Yes, and I'm sure leaving with Vivienne in tow did not help either."

I snorted. "No, it did not help at all."

"I'll meet you inside the reception. I just have one more thing I need to do before I join the ceremony."

He slapped my shoulder, then walked toward one of the unlit

hallways near the rear of the basement. My father's generation was one of the last to live in the shadows, hiding from humans. Sometimes, I think he still feels most comfortable there, though. Especially when we feel threatened with the risk of discovery.

I walked back the way I came with Vivienne and nearly bumped into her when I turned the corner.

"What are you still doing here?" I asked her, annoyed but not surprised to find her there.

"I'm coming with you to Norway."

"What? No, absolutely not—you weren't supposed to hear any of that."

"Yes, well, I did, and now I'm coming. You can't go alone, Hunter."

"I won't. I'll be taking Thomas with me."

"Thomas has to take care of manticore business while you're away."

"Tony, then."

"Tony has the diplomatic skills of a boar."

She was right. Tony would not be the right manticore for this mission. Neither of us mentioned Leo—that was intentional, I was sure of it.

"You need me, Hunter. I have connections in Norway. I can ask questions without it looking suspicious. Let me come. I want to help you."

I didn't want Vivienne's help, but she was right, I needed it. Suddenly the idea of lying to Michaela and running off to Norway with Vivienne seemed a lot less favorable, but my reasons were still the same—I needed to protect my family.

"Fine. But you need to take a separate flight to Norway. I do not want anyone to see us leaving together. I won't do that to Michaela."

A triumphant smile spread across Vivienne's face. Her white teeth gleamed in the dark basement. She stuck out her hand, "Deal?"

I stared at it and reluctantly raised mine to shake it. "Deal."

A nagging feeling grew in the pit of my stomach. Standing in the deep, dark, underground, and shaking the hand of a woman who had already betrayed me, I prayed I hadn't just struck a deal with the devil.

***

When Vivienne and I returned to the ballroom, I spotted Michaela at the podium. Her cheeks flushed, and she beamed at the crowd applauding her. When some students stood up, the rest of the room followed. Her cheeks grew brighter. I smiled at her discomfort and my heart swelled with pride. By the looks of it, I had missed quite a speech. I hadn't even known she would be a speaker tonight. Perhaps Michaela kept things from me as well. The thought made me frown, but I recovered quickly when our eyes locked. She held my gaze and her smile faltered a bit when her eyes moved to the woman beside me. *Dammit, Vivienne was still here.*

I turned to her. "I'll see you tomorrow. It's best if we part ways now." She nodded and walked away; I didn't bother to see in which direction she went. My focus zeroed in on Michaela.

I quickened my step to meet her as soon as she walked off the podium. Reaching, I pulled her in close to me and whispered in her ear. "I didn't know you were speaking tonight."

She shrugged and said, "Neither did I," and looked past my shoulder. I followed her gaze and caught Laura giving Michaela a quick thumbs up. *Ah, I should have guessed Laura was behind this.*

"What did your father have to say?" she asked and intertwined her fingers with mine. I swallowed and began with the truth.

"He needs me to take care of some manticore business out of town. I have to leave in the morning."

"It must be urgent."

"It is."

"Confidential too since you met with him in private."

I let out a breath, relieved that she understood. "Yes."

"But Vivienne was privy to the information?"

I faltered because she wasn't exactly part of the conversation, but she had overheard it. "My father had asked her to leave."

"Mmm..."

"I won't be gone for long, a few days maybe. I'll be back before the end of the week."

"What sort of business needs to be kept hidden from everyone?"

This was a tough one to answer without lying, but I did my best. "One of the most important rules of the Manticore Kingdom is to keep our existence a secret. Manticores are accustomed to secrets, sometimes even from each other. Keeping secrets has kept us alive. My father understands that the fewer who know about the situation, the safer everyone will be."

"Secrets even from your wife?"

"If it means protecting her—then yes."

"I don't want that kind of relationship, Hunter. I want us to be truthful, all the time."

"I am not keeping anything from you that concerns you directly. This is manticore business and I must follow my king's orders. I need you to understand."

Her imploring eyes looked away from mine for a few minutes. She seemed to scan the room until her gaze narrowed on someone and she remained still.

"Fine. Just one more question."

"What is it?"

"What's Vivienne's last name?"

"Vivienne's last name? Why would you want to know that?"

She smiled, but it unsettled me rather than reassured me.

"Oh, just curious."

Deciding it wasn't worth the argument, she'd probably find out anyway, I told her. "Barros. Vivienne Barros."

She nodded and walked back to our table. A smile remained on her face for the rest of the evening, but something felt off. The sooner I could take care of this manticore problem, the better.

Three

Michaela

Hunter was lying to me; I was sure of it. I didn't doubt his conversation with his father was about manticore business, but I would bet it had nothing to do with land development. I didn't know why he kept pushing me away, but I wouldn't accept it. After Hunter left this morning, I spent an hour on my phone googling the name Vivienne Barros, while making breakfast for Violet and me and came up with nothing.

I was holding Violet against my hip and the phone against my ear when the doorbell rang. It was my grandmother, Ramona. After Violet was born, she and my Aunt Julie moved into our condo building. They wanted to be closer to us and I couldn't be more grateful.

"Thanks for coming, *Nonna,*" I said and closed the apartment door behind my grandmother. The little ten-month-old in my arms was just as delighted to see her great-grandmother—her legs swung wildly and her butt bounced on my hip as she squealed, "nanana."

"*Oh, piccolina! Vieni qua!*" My grandmother stretched her arms toward Violet and my little girl flung herself into them. I smiled, then adjusted the phone next to my ear and continued to wait.

"Whom are you talking to?" my grandmother asked.

"Um, I'm on hold with the Academy."

My grandmother shrugged and continued to coo at Violet. "Look what *Nonna* brought you today." She pulled out a string of violet beads.

"Oh, are those teething beads?" I asked.

"No," she said and frowned. "What are teething beads?"

"Never mind. Isn't she a little young for jewelry then?" I laughed.

My grandmother shook her head. "These are not jewelry; these are protection beads."

"Protection?"

"Yes, they were my great-grandmother's. She had used them to fight a vicious manticore in England and won. She gave them to me and now I'm passing them on to *Violetta*."

I walked over to touch the beads. They were smooth like gemstones. Violet immediately shoved them into her mouth and drooled all over them. "I think Violet prefers them as teething beads."

I chuckled again, but my grandmother kept trying to pull the beads from Violet's mouth but finally gave up when Violet's little fist clenched the beads and she rubbed them against her gums.

"Yes, hello, this is Michaela Durand... no problem." I sighed as the receptionist put me back on hold.

"Michaela, aren't you going to be late for your meeting with your new client?" I still ran my own PR company while teaching a course part-time at the Academy.

"Yes, but I've been on hold for ten minutes and I don't want to risk dropping the call in the elevator."

A voice on the other end of the line introduced herself as Kira and apologized for the wait.

"Hi Kira, can you kindly connect me to Professor Wallace's office?"

"Oh, of course, Ms. Durand. It's just been so hectic. I'll transfer you right away."

Kira wasted no time transferring the call. A moment later, Professor Wallace answered his office phone.

"This is Professor Wallace."

"Professor Wallace, hi, it's me, Michaela."

"Michaela, how are you?" His question loaded with concern.

I tried to calm my voice as it did sound a bit panicked and I didn't want Professor Wallace suspicious of my motivation. I only wanted to find out if he had any further information about Hunter's mission.

"Oh, I'm fine. Just running late as usual, so a bit frazzled."

"Glad to hear everything is all right."

"I'm sorry to bother you. I was just wondering if I could come by the office later and chat with you about a few things. It won't be until after hours, though, is that okay?"

"Certainly. I will be working late tonight; we are short-staffed right now."

"Okay, great, I appreciate you taking the time to chat with me."

"No problem, Michaela. Anytime."

I exhaled, relieved that I would get a chance to ask Professor Wallace about some of my suspicions in private. Wanting to pay him back for his help, I wondered if perhaps I could return the favor. "I have meetings all day today, but I can come by tomorrow afternoon to help around the Academy if you need it, Professor. I'm sure my grandmother will be happy to babysit again."

I caught a glimpse of my grandmother's enthusiastic nod. She leaned down and kissed Violet on the top of her head.

"That would be wonderful, Michaela. Thank you."

"No problem. Why is it you're short-staffed, anyway? Did someone quit?"

"Oh, no, nothing like that. One of our research assistants left for Norway this morning, so we just need a little help for the next few days."

I stood still in my kitchen. For a moment, I couldn't utter a word.

"Norway?" I finally spit out.

"Yes, it was last minute, but she said it was important."

"She?"

"Yes, Vivienne. You may have met her at the graduation last night."

An image of Hunter and Vivienne walking away from me, side by side, popped into my head.

"Yes, I did, briefly." I leaned forward on the counter, my brown curls brushing against the white countertop.

"Well, she said she would be back in a few days, so again, I appreciate your offer."

"No problem, professor. I'll see you later tonight." I ended the call before hearing his response.

I found myself seated on the couch but didn't remember taking the steps to get there. I slumped down and covered my face with my hands.

"Michaela, *bella*, what's the matter?" My grandmother's voice was only a few feet away, but it sounded muffled in my head. *Hunter lied to me.*

I opened my mouth to rant and rave, but nothing came out. Was I being dramatic? Maybe, but Hunter not telling me about Vivienne felt like a betrayal.

My grandmother placed Violet in her playpen and sat down beside me, rubbing my back. "You look very pale, Michaela. What could the professor have told you to make you this upset?"

"He told me that Vivienne left for Norway."

"Who's Vivienne? Is she a friend of yours?"

"No, she's Hunter's ex-girlfriend."

"Why does it matter that Vivienne went to...oh." She stopped mid-sentence and stood up. She paced the room with her hands on her hips.

"I thought Hunter went to Norway on business. Is this Vivienne part of the company now?"

"No. But Hunter only said that he was going for business. I don't think that's the real reason."

"Why do you think he really went?"

"Last night, Leo told me about a mauling in Norway that reminded him of a manticore attack. I think Hunter went to investigate."

"But why not tell you the truth?"

I shook my head. "I don't know why he would bring Vivienne and not me," I shouted, angry he would leave me behind.

My grandmother stopped pacing. I glanced up, and she was now nodding vigorously. "I understand."

"You do?"

"Of course. Hunter is trying to protect you?"

"Protect me? I'm the one with the power to control manticores. He doesn't need to protect me."

"Hunter will always put protecting you first, Michaela. I am sure of it. And he's right. You have a daughter now. You need to protect her."

"Violet is safe and protected here, with you, her goddess of a grandmother and her manticore family. Hunter is there with some woman, while the one person who can truly protect him is me and I'm nearly four thousand miles away." Frustrated by the distance and my concern, I shot up from the couch and resumed my grandmother's pacing.

"Michaela, please. Let Hunter handle it. Let the manticores sort out their own problems, don't get involved."

I shook my head. "You and I will never agree on this, I know."

Fisting my hands beside me, I continued. "But *Nonna*, manticores are my business. Like you, I am a Shed woman, born with the power to control a manticore's heart and mind. If there is a manticore threatening humans or other manticores, it is my responsibility to do something about it. I cannot ignore it." The blood of an Egyptian god ran through my veins, and at that moment, I felt the power surge within me.

"You sound just like your mother," she whispered, but I heard it.

"That's not the first time someone has said that, but it's the first time I'd agree with it. But, unlike my mother, I don't plan to go about this alone."

My grandmother raised her eyebrow at me. "Who will you take? Leo? Laura?"

I shook my head and hesitated for only a moment. I grabbed my phone and dialed a number I hadn't called in months. The phone rang, and a voice answered, "Michaela, is that you?" The voice was gravelly and concern laced in its tone.

"Yes, it's me."

"Is everything all right?"

I looked up, and my eyes connected with my grandmother. "I need your help."

There was a pause on the other end, then the voice said, "Anything."

"Will you meet me in Oslo tomorrow?"

"Norway?"

"Yes. I'll text you the name of the hotel."

"What's happened?"

"There may be some trouble. Will you come anyway?"

"I'll be there."

"Thank you."

"Wait! Does Hunter know you're calling me? Will he be there?"

"He's already there, but he doesn't know I'm coming."

The voice went silent on the other end for two seconds. Then, "I'll see you tomorrow."

"I'll see you then." I pulled the phone away from my ear and ended the call.

"Michaela, *bella*, I really hope you know what you're doing."

Me too.

"Can you stay here with Violet, *Nonna*?" I asked, placing my hand on her forearm, stopping her from picking up Violet.

"Yes, of course. Just please, be careful." She patted my hand.

"I know what I'm doing. I've dealt with crazy manticores before." But my confidence wavered a bit. "How hard can it be this time?"

My grandmother shook her head and muttered to herself in Italian.

Four

Michaela

Centuries ago, manticores hid their kingdom from humans beneath Central Park and have kept their dungeons, courts, and academy undetected there ever since. I parked my car in the gated lot above the Manticore Kingdom and took the private elevator down to the bottom floor. The familiar, dark wood-paneled hallways lined with portraits of manticore scholars comforted me as I walked toward Professor Wallace's office. His door was slightly opened, but I knocked anyway.

"Michaela, come in," he called from his leather upholstered chair. The professor wore his usual sports jacket with velour elbow patches. This one was green with yellow pinstripes.

"Thank you for waiting for me, Professor." I took a seat in front of his desk and unbuttoned my black blazer.

"As I said, it's not a problem. Besides, you'll be helping me too."

I groaned inwardly but squared my shoulders. "About that."

The professor leaned back in his chair. "You won't be able to help?"

"I'm so sorry Professor Wallace, but I need to go to Norway."

"Why is everyone running off to Norway?"

I lowered my eyes to stare at the desk's antique legs, carved to resemble a lion's paw. "I can't tell you."

He shook his head but didn't press further. Maybe Hunter was right and manticores accepted secrets better than humans did.

"All right. What can I do for you?"

"Is there anything I should know about the manticores from Norway?"

Professor Wallace shook his head again. "No, there's nothing particular about manticores in Norway. They are the same as those of us here in New York – only perhaps they enjoy the snow a bit more than we do," he chuckled. As a Torontonian, I felt the same way about disliking the snow.

"Okay, that's good to know. I didn't want to arrive in Norway unprepared for a gang of blood-thirsty manticores."

Professor Wallace smiled. "We are not vampires but we do have a temper, I'll give you that."

"Thanks, Professor. I'll get out of your way now."

I stood and nearly reached the office door when the professor called out to me, "Hold on, Michaela."

I turned. "Yes?"

"There *is* something I should warn you about," he said, steepling his fingers underneath his chin.

"Is it Norway's knighted penguin?" I grinned. "I read all about him in the news."

"No, no. Not that," he said with a frown. "But I wouldn't laugh about him, he's a skilled military creature."

I waited for Professor Wallace to wink at me, but he didn't. He must be serious about the penguin. I guess I shouldn't be surprised.

"We have magistrates all over the world that handle manticore business in their own country, but the king oversees them all. So, if Vivienne left for Norway yesterday and now you plan to leave too, for reasons you cannot say, I assume there's some trouble with manticores there."

I snapped out of my musing, pulled from his quick deduction, but I didn't respond. I simply stared back at him, but Professor Wallace nodded once. "That's what I thought. You need to be careful, Michaela."

"You are the second person to say this to me today."

"Then I hope you're listening."

"I can take care of myself, Professor. I've been doing a pretty good job of it so far."

"Yes, you have, and I'm glad of it. While there isn't anything intrinsically different about them, the Norwegian manticores are strong and they are loyal. Many Viking kings were manticores, so their gene to dominate is quite potent. If you find yourself in a situation where you must reveal your power, make sure you do not leave any survivors."

"Why would you say that?"

"I am certain there are several families there who would be thrilled to possess a weapon like you."

"No one can possess me, Professor."

"Not willingly no, but you have a weakness now, Michaela."

My heart jolted in my chest. The thought of someone taking Violet from me made the hair on the back of my neck stand up.

"If they threaten your daughter, you will do anything they ask. Do you deny it?"

I couldn't, so I shook my head.

"Do not show them who you are, or what you can do. If they do find out, run, and never let them catch you."

"I understand. Thank you, professor."

"Be safe, Michaela."

I nodded again, buttoned up my black blazer, and walked out the professor's door. Images of Violet kidnapped or hurt threatened to undo me, but I pulled myself together. By the time I arrived home, I felt calmer. However, when I held my baby girl in my arms, the tears I so valiantly held back in the professor's office fell freely and swiftly from my eyes. For a moment, I second-guessed leaving for

Norway. Perhaps my place was here, holding Violet. But the thought of Hunter battling some crazy manticore with only Vivienne by his side solidified my decision. I wasn't sure if this rogue manticore worked alone, but I would not leave Hunter by himself to find out. A higher power gave me these gifts, and I was going to use them. It was just so damn hard to leave her behind.

A warm touch on my shoulder startled me, and I pulled Violet closer to my chest as she slept.

"You're crying?" my grandmother asked.

I balanced the baby in my arms to wipe away my tears. "Yes. I'm having a hard time leaving her behind. I'm scared she'll need me."

My grandmother caressed Violet's forehead while I held her. "I would do anything for her," she whispered. "I've never had to use my powers and never wanted to. But if anyone tries to hurt her, I'll use all the chants in my possession to stop their beating heart. I promise you this, Michaela."

The fierceness in her voice broke me, and tears streamed down my face again. I knew how much those words cost my grandmother—a woman who left her family because she refused to fight manticores.

Closing my eyes, I leaned down and kissed Violet's forehead. "Mama will be back soon," I said and gently placed her in the crib.

"Thank you," I said to my grandmother, my hand on her forearm. Then I left her with Violet to finish packing.

***

The next morning, I boarded the plane and brought a few of my mother's books with me to study some newer chants. When I finally disembarked, the city's beauty struck me. The breathtaking mountains and cold, fresh air infused life into my lungs. As though the air was steeped in magic, there was something mystical in the scenery around me.

I arrived at The Oslo Regency Hotel just before eight at night.

Being May, the sun was still high in the sky. I was told in the summer months it could be daylight for more than twenty hours. Checking my watch, I had about an hour before my meeting in the lobby. It would be just enough time to shower and unpack.

It surprised me to find hardwood floors across my hotel room instead of carpet and white marble throughout the bathroom tiles and countertop. I walked over to the window and drew the curtains. A brown and green mountain range crested over the neighborhood. Their beauty and size were majestic. Turning back around, I glimpsed at the clock near the bed and hurried into the bathroom. Even though there was a tub, I opted for a quick shower. The warm water sluiced down my body and relaxed my tense muscles. I massaged the back of my neck and turned up the temperature of the water. Steady rivulets trickled down my face and I gulped in a deep breath and a bit of water, too. It had been about ten months since I'd showered without listening for Violet's cry or worrying if she were too quiet that she must have swallowed a toy or something. I let myself decompress one muscle at a time until I wiggled my toes and lifted my face, the gentle spray massaging my tired eyes. About thirty minutes later, when the water temperature had cooled, I finally got out.

While the extra time in the shower was necessary to unwind, I may have lingered to prepare myself for the meeting. I took extra time to blow dry my hair with a round brush and put some lipstick on, too. I felt guilty for calling him here. Months ago, I told him I didn't need him anymore and yet he was the first person I called when I needed help. I hoped he would understand.

I dressed in a pair of jeans and a white T-shirt and took the elevators down to the lobby. I spotted him as soon as I turned the corner. His hair was just as close-cropped as the last time I saw him, and the familiarity made me smile. I walked closer to him, but he hadn't spotted me yet. I got close enough to him to tap him on the shoulder. He immediately spun around and his eyes grew large and his smile even broader.

"Michaela!" he shouted and pulled me into his arms. It felt good, and it felt right.

"I missed you," he whispered into my ear, and I fought to hold back my tears.

"I missed you too, Nicholas."

Five

Hunter

I tried calling Michaela once more this afternoon, but it went straight to voicemail again. I spoke to her last night, and she'd said everything was fine, but I wasn't convinced. Perhaps I was projecting, but I couldn't shake the feeling that she was keeping something from me.

"Are you ready to go?" I asked Vivienne as I placed my phone in my back pocket.

She sucked in her bottom lip, her white teeth raking her red lipstick. "I'm ready."

We walked through the front doors of our hotel and into my rental, parked just in front.

After driving a little more than half an hour along the southern coast, Vivienne pointed to a dirt road up ahead. "Make a right over here."

A cloud of dust swirled behind us as I checked the rearview mirror.

Astrid Nilsen lived in a modest house that resembled a cabin flanked by tall trees, trimmed with a wooden porch, and the absence of neighbors. Some of the older manticores never wanted to assimilate and preferred to stay alone. Astrid was one of the oldest manticores I knew and she had always preferred her solitude. That's why I found it strange when my father chose her as the magistrate of Norway. He said he trusted Astrid and knew she would handle problems efficiently because she had no problem "sending everyone back whence they came".

Gravel crunched beneath the tires as I came to a stop in front of the house.

Astrid stood on her porch with her arms crossed over her chest. Her long blonde hair was tied back into a braid, and she wore brown leather pants and a cream cashmere sweater.

"Astrid. It is nice to see you again," I said, climbing up the stairs. I had met Astrid only once before. It was in New York and she wore a scowl on her face the whole time. I thought she hated the city, but it may just be her usual demeanor.

Astrid narrowed her eyes at the woman beside me, and I hoped to answer her unspoken question. "This is Vivienne. She's here to assist me."

"I heard you married. Is she your wife?"

"No, Michaela's at home. Vivienne is here because she is familiar with a few of the manticore families in this region."

"Good. Then she can make the introductions."

"I'll be happy to," said Vivienne.

"Come inside, both of you. I'll tell you everything I know, then we can figure out what needs to be done about this situation."

I followed Astrid inside her home. Only a few pieces of furniture stood in the room, but they were sufficient. There was an absence of any knickknacks or throw pillows or anything one might purchase to add distinction to one's home. Except for a spear that hung over the fireplace. I stood staring at the weapon, mesmerized by the intricate design forged in its blade, when Astrid said, "It was my great grandfather's. He gave it to me when I became a magistrate. He said it was to remind me that although I could solve most problems through diplomacy, some manticores only responded to strength. I've never had to use it—yet."

"It sounds like your grandfather and I have a lot in common." I reached over to touch the spear. It was cold, and I shivered from the contact.

"I also think it's haunted, but he would never confirm it."

"You could have warned me," I muttered and Astrid shrugged.

"What can I offer you to drink?" she asked, walking toward her kitchen.

"Whatever you have is fine." I strode over to the table and sat down. Vivienne pulled out a chair and joined me. I blended in with the cabin with my dark jeans and grey sweater, but Vivienne stuck out with her tight-fitted red dress.

Astrid passed us two beers; not bothering with a bottle opener since it was unnecessary. I lifted the bottle and gulped down a healthy amount while Vivienne pouted and reached for a glass in the drying rack.

"Astrid, tell me about the second attack. Was it similar to the first one?"

"No, but I'm certain it was the same manticore."

"Why is that?"

"Despite our conquering ancestors, Norwegians are not violent people. They are peaceful and happy for the most part." Astrid sat down in front of me at the table, her hand wrapped around her drink.

"When I first heard about the attack, I worried that a manticore met with an aggressive human and could not control his own instinct to dominate. Perhaps it was an argument that turned violent unexpectedly."

"You thought it could have been an accident?" asked Vivienne.

"No. I *hoped* it was an accident, but it was immediately obvious that it wasn't."

I took a swig of my beer and Astrid did the same before she continued. "First, the attack was brutal. The cut went deeper than any accidental swipe could have gone. In fact, the claws went straight through the man's spinal cord."

I cringed and instinctively moved my hand to my abdomen.

"He didn't stop there. Even after immobilizing the victim, he continued to attack—the face, the neck, even his groin."

I crossed my legs. "And the second attack?"

"Same as the first. Except this time, it was a woman."

"Bastard," whispered Vivienne.

"Yes, and we need to stop him before he attacks again," said Astrid.

"What's your plan?" I leaned forward, but Astrid moved back and folded her arms.

"I've been the magistrate in these parts for more than a hundred years and I've only seen something this brutal once before. I don't want to see it ever again. We take care of this problem once and for all. We should start with the club district tonight. Both attacks happened after one in the morning and outside of a bar. We need to separate so we can cover as many bars as possible. I've written the addresses and which ones I will take."

"What are we looking for exactly?"

"A manticore with a fresh wound. They found a knife next to the last victim, but she had no cuts on her body. We suspect the weapon was hers and she may have gotten a swipe in before the manticore overpowered her. There were traces of blood that were not the victims."

"Did the lab examine that blood? It could be dangerous for the technicians if they inadvertently discover the venom inside the sample."

"We already took care of stealing the evidence and replacing it with a sample that will come back inconclusive."

"Good work, Astrid," I said.

"Are the Pedersens still the most influential family here in Oslo?" Vivienne asked, surprising me with her knowledge.

"Yes. Those manticores have not lost their place as the richest and most prominent family in this city."

Rubbing her chin, Vivienne asked, "Wasn't there some trouble with one of the Pedersen boys a few years back?"

"Yes, but we handled that, and there's been no trouble there since," explained Astrid. "The ones we need to look more closely at are the Larsens."

"I haven't heard of them," I said, but Vivienne pursed her lips.

"They've made some noise, maybe not loud enough to be heard across the pond, but they've been making moves."

"Moves?" I asked.

"The Larsen family is making a move for the top spot in terms of manticore influence here in Norway." Astrid placed her palm on the round wooden table in front of us. "The Pedersen family organizes grand fundraisers, helps build hospitals and universities. They are the most well-known and respected family around here."

"So, the Larsens are trying to do the same now?" I asked.

"No. They appear to have a different strategy," explained Astrid. "The Larsens are not into charity or building communities like the Pedersens. No, they're interested in making money and offering favors in exchange for power."

When my eyes narrowed, Astrid continued. "They look for businesses that are failing and buy them out only to rebuild a stronger brand. They have hired the most financially savvy manticores and have built a company that appears to have the Midas touch—whatever they touch turns to gold. It has caught the Pedersen family's attention but the Larsens have broken no rules so my hands are tied to stop them."

"If they're attracting unwanted attention, they're bending the kingdom's rules," I explained.

"They divided the company into many sectors. No one in the human world has noticed—only those of us aware of a manticore's abilities."

"It appears the need to dominate has evolved our abilities into a different ruthless beast. One who seeks to rule with his wealth."

"Yes," said Astrid, her face grimacing as though she'd just bitten into a lemon.

"We need to speak with the head of the Larsen household tonight. Where would we find him?"

"Well, since they own one of the trendiest nightclubs in Oslo, I would imagine you shall find one of them there this evening."

"Where is it located?" I asked.

"Just down the street from the last attack."

Vivienne turned to look at me. "This could be it. It's falling into place," she said.

I shook my head, still confused about the motive. "Why would attacking two humans help them gain wealth?"

"Glen Larsen is the mayor of Oslo. He controls the government," explained Astrid. "The first victim was a retired police officer and the second an airport security officer. If they can control both the government and police, they'd be the strongest family in town. No matter how many fundraisers the Pedersens throw, they could not compete with the power the Larsens would hold."

"So, this is all just a turf war, a battle for power?"

"Yes, it looks that way," said Astrid. "And you just landed in the middle of it."

While Astrid's theory made sense, it felt like I was still missing an important piece to this puzzle. If Larsen's motive was power, why resort to murder? Why now? Why in such a dramatic fashion as to catch the attention of the king in New York? It made little sense, but I was going to visit this club tonight and find out more.

I stood from the table. "Thank you for taking the time to speak with us, Astrid," I said, walking down the hallway toward the front porch. Shaking Astrid's hand, I added, "We'll stay in touch."

"You do that," she said and closed the door.

As we walked back to the car, Vivienne turned to me and said, "I know one of the Larsen boys."

I smiled. If I were to call up Larsen, it may set him off, but if Vivienne called him, that would be less suspicious. "You know, I thought I would regret bringing you with me to Norway, but maybe not."

She smiled, her red lips curling away from her straight teeth. "You didn't bring me, Hunter. I volunteered." She shoved me out of the way and opened the car door. She turned her head back and smiled, "And you're welcome."

As she climbed in, I laughed. I never thought I would laugh at anything Vivienne had to say again. It felt good, like I had finally forgiven her for sleeping with my cousin, John.

Six

Michaela

"Why are you crying, Michaela?" Nicholas asked as he wiped away the tear on my cheek. His hands had brown spots on them I'd never noticed before and his hair had more salt than pepper to it now. He pulled out the chair next to him and I sat down.

"I guess I'm just happy to see you and overwhelmed that you would travel all this way for me even though it may be dangerous," I said and pulled out a tissue to wipe the rest of my face. I patted underneath my eyes and Nicholas's bright smile kept the rest of my tears at bay.

"I made a vow to help the Sheds, but even if that were not the case, I would be here for you. You are family to me."

It was true. Nicholas was like a father to me.

"Thank you, Nicholas. Even though we have not spoken in months, you were the first person I thought of when I needed help and the only one I can trust with this information."

"You can always count on me." He reached for my hand and squeezed it. "Now tell me, what's going on?"

"I know little, only that there was a mauling here in Norway two days ago. It must have been pretty bad, or there was some sort of sign of it being a manticore attack for Hunter to travel all the way here and not tell me about it."

"I think you're right. Before I left, I asked Adam and Olivia to look into any police reports in Oslo that looked suspicious. I told her to send the information to you. I am still not very good with the technical stuff."

"That was a great idea," I said and sighed a breath of relief that we had a team of people helping us. "How's Adam?"

"Oh, Adam is his usual grouchy self. He's fine," said Nicholas and waved off my concern.

"Have you ever been to Norway?" I asked.

"No, this is my first time. I'm familiar with some hotels and streets, however. I helped your mother track down a manticore here once on one of her missions, but she wouldn't let me come. She preferred to work alone." Nicholas shrugged his shoulders and looked away. "She caught the rogue in just two days so I couldn't really argue with her."

"Well, I'm happy to get all the help you can give," I smiled and Nicholas beamed at me.

My phone pinged, and I rummaged through my purse to get it. "This could be from Olivia." But when I checked, the message was from Hunter. I had several missed calls from him, but this was the first text message. "It's not her. Excuse me for a second." I typed a brief message back.

Me: Everything is fine. Sorry, I missed your call, reception is terrible. I'll call you later.

As soon as I sent the message, three dots appeared underneath then Hunter replied immediately.

Hunter: I'm glad you're all right. How's Violet? I miss you both.

Me: She's good and we miss you too. I've got to go, chat later.

Hunter liked the message but didn't reply. Relieved, I didn't want him to ask anything I couldn't answer truthfully. I was about to put my phone away when an email notification flashed on top of my screen. "Oh, this must be from Olivia."

I opened the app and saw two new emails from her. "She sent me two police reports." I opened the latest one since I hadn't heard about this second attack. I frowned. "It's about a missing person." Why would Olivia send me this? I checked Olivia's message. "I'm including the second email because the woman's family said the last place someone saw her was at a bar only a kilometer from the last attack. I thought it could be related." *Good thinking, Olivia.* I opened the first police report, and this one described the mauling Leo had mentioned.

"God help us," the words jumped from my mouth and I covered my lips with my fingers. I passed Nicholas the phone to read it because I couldn't bring myself to describe the details of the assault.

Nicholas's eyebrows pulled together, and he rubbed his forehead as he reviewed the report. "This is the worst attack I've ever read. No wonder Hunter left immediately."

I nodded and my mind raced, thinking what we should do next. "Does it mention any witnesses?"

Nicholas used his finger to scroll to the end of the report. "No, I don't see anything here."

"Then we need to figure out where his next victim will be. I'm sure there will be another. That attack was not personal. He wanted someone's attention and now he has ours." I tapped a finger to my lips. "We just need him to show himself."

"How can he show himself if we don't even know what he looks like?" asked Nicholas.

A smile spread across my lips. "I don't need to know what he looks like because I know what he sounds like." I tapped my breastbone.

Nicholas' eyes widened, and he slapped the table with his hand. "Of course! You will listen for their heartbeat."

"Yes."

But then his forehead creased. "But won't the bar be too loud?"

I frowned because he was right. I probably couldn't hear a manticore's heartbeat over the loud music. "Then I'll have to think of something else. I've been around manticores for nearly a year. I've gotten good at spotting one. They are usually quiet in larger groups, not looking to attract attention. Most humans instinctively stay away, so they may be alone in a crowd."

"Obviously, there are the amber eyes," said Nicholas.

"Yup. While most are amber colored, some have brown with just a ring of amber around the iris."

"You're not planning to get that close to a rogue manticore, are you?"

"I don't have much choice."

"Couldn't you use a chant in the ancient books to control their minds? Make them do something like raise their hand?"

"I could, but I would attract too much attention. Everyone would wonder what just happened. No. My instincts tell me to track and observe. I'm sure that's how my mother did it. We need to start with the bars in the area. He's looking for a victim. The question is, how does he choose one? If it's not gender, it's got to be something else."

I read the reports again. *Were these random attacks or did the victims have something in common?* I wrote the first victim's name, Jan Olsen, down on a napkin, then searched it online. A newspaper article from two days ago described the victim as a retired police officer. I reconsidered whether the attack was impersonal or had the officer arrested the rogue in the past? If so, why attack him now? When I searched the woman's name, Evelyn Berg, there was no newspaper article about her. But I found a Facebook account. Based on a few of her posts, she looked to be in her late fifties. I searched through all her photos and even checked up on her friends. However, I found no connection between the missing woman and the murdered man.

"It looks to be random," I said, rubbing my forehead. Where do I look now? Not knowing the connection makes preventing the next attack that much harder.

Nicholas frowned too. He brought his fingers to his lips and his eyes narrowed in on my necklace. "You said your grandmother gave you that necklace before your wedding?"

"Actually, my aunt Julie gave it to me. But, yes, it belonged to my *Nonna*. Why?"

"Your mother's books say amulets help strengthen a Shed's power. But not just any amulet. I suspect this may be one of the special ones."

"I did clutch it while fighting Elenora's army. It helped strengthen my powers."

Nicholas stared at the amulet as though the gem could tell its secrets. "Try listening for a manticore's heartbeat in this room."

I nodded and closed my eyes. I heard soft jazz music playing in the background of the lobby bar. Murmured conversations hummed around me and a woman laughed to my left. I strained harder but couldn't hear anything that resembled a heartbeat. "Either I can't hear anything or there aren't any manticores around."

"Try again, but this time, hold on to your amulet."

I curled my fingers around my necklace and leaned forward, placing my elbows on the table. I tried to shut all the background noise into a separate compartment and listened for anything else.

Nothing.

I shook my head and lifted my arms off the table. "I don't hear—"

"Try it again, Michaela," insisted Nicholas. "This time, imagine the amulet as a heart, pumping blood and beating inside the palm of your hand."

I tilted my head to see if Nicholas was serious, and when his face did not change, I tried what he suggested. I grasped the amulet and envisioned it as a beating heart. It pumped rhythmically in my mind. *Ba-boom, ba-boom.* This is silly. It's not working. I squeezed my eyes and the amulet in my hand harder. *Ba-ba-boom, Ba-ba-boom.* Wait! That was the sound of a manticore's heartbeat. I listened for it again. *Ba-ba-boom, Ba-ba-boom.* There it was!

I opened my eyes and smiled, "Nicholas!" I said. "It worked."

"It did?" he asked, surprised. Then his eyes grew bigger. The same thought must have popped into his head too. I frantically scanned the room, and Nicholas turned in his chair to do the same. When a man near the door stood up and quickly left the bar, I didn't hesitate. I grabbed my purse and followed him.

"Michaela, wait!" called Nicholas behind me, but I didn't slow down. A tall man with brown hair, wearing a black leather jacket and black jeans, hurried through the hotel lobby and toward the front doors. I quickened my step to catch up to him but held back from a full-out run. When he walked through the front doors, he turned right and I sprinted after him. Pushing the heavy glass door, I heaved it out of the way and turned right as well. A busy street filled with pedestrians engulfed me and I momentarily lost him. I snagged a glimpse of his jacket just as he bent forward and slid into the passenger seat of a car.

"Excuse me," I said, having bumped into a burly man on the street. I tried to catch the license plate of the vehicle, but it was too late. The white car was gone and so was the manticore.

"What happened?" Nicholas asked, panting when he caught up to me.

"I lost him." I stared out into the street, hoping I would spot the car, but nothing.

"The chances that it was actually our rogue manticore are slim. It was probably just another regular manticore."

"You're right. At least now I know I can focus and listen for their heartbeat—right before I crush it." A smile spread across my face, and Nicholas chuckled.

"You know, you really are frightening underneath all that sweetness."

"Thank you," I said and grinned.

"You remind me of—"

"Don't say it!" I warned him. While I had no bad will against my mother, I still hated when people compared me to her. But he just shook his head and smirked the entire way back to the hotel. "Time to get ready to go clubbing tonight."

The smirk fell from Nicholas's face, and I couldn't hold back mine.

Seven

Hunter

Vivienne had called Alexander Larsen soon after leaving Astrid's house and had told him she'd be in town for a few days. He'd wasted no time inviting her to his club tonight for a drink. With that settled, we returned to our separate hotel rooms to ready ourselves. Before I left for the evening, though, I tried calling Michaela again. Her phone went straight to voicemail. *What's going on? Is she purposely avoiding my call?* I tried calling the apartment next.

"Hello?"

"Ramona, hi, it's Hunter," I said. I could hear Violet babbling in the background, and the sound comforted me and relieved some of my anxiety. "Is Michaela at home? She isn't answering her cell phone, and I'm concerned." I left out the part where I worried she was avoiding me.

"Oh, nothing to worry about, Hunter. She's fine," said Ramona. I ran my hand through my hair and paced the carpeted hotel room floor. "All right. I'm glad to hear everything is fine. When she gets home, can you ask her to call me? I've only received a brief text from her all day and that's not like her."

"I will. I'm sure she'll call soon," said Ramona. Her light tone gave me some relief. If there was something wrong with Michaela, Ramona would have said something. "Give Violet a kiss for me. I'll be back in a few days."

"Be safe, Hunter," she said and hung up the phone. I stared at my cell phone for a second. Why would she say 'be safe' when she thought I was away for business? Was that just a general 'be safe' or did she know more? As soon as I could speak to Michaela, I would tell her everything. The hell with this secrecy stuff. I was driving myself crazy, analyzing why she wasn't answering my calls and why Ramona was telling me to 'be safe'. I was coming clean to Michaela tonight... as soon as I finally got a hold of her.

***

A steel gate wrapped around the front of the bar, hugging the club-goers while they waited to enter *Lexi's*. The cab dropped off Vivienne and me out front and I buttoned up my jacket as soon as I climbed out of the backseat. The air had cooled significantly at night and I frowned at Vivienne's bare shoulders as I helped her out of the car. "Are you going to be all right without a jacket? Do you want mine?"

She eyed the jacket, her gaze lingering on my chest. "Maybe later, I'm fine right now. Besides, it will be warm inside the club."

"You're probably right," I said and walked us toward the back of the line.

"Alexander told me to come to the entrance on the east side of the building," said Vivienne, turning to her right. When I followed her, she stopped me with a hand to my chest. "I'm going in alone. We need to cover as many clubs as possible on this strip, so while I'm inside at *Lexi's*, you should go to the one over there." She pointed to a bar two doors down from where we stood.

"It doesn't feel right leaving you here alone. I'll come in, make sure Alexander is not our killer, then I'll go."

Vivienne rolled her eyes. "If Alexander sees you with me, he's going to think I set him up to be interrogated and close up. I don't need a bodyguard. Now go."

I didn't argue. Vivienne was right, she could take care of herself.

"Call or text if you need backup," I said, and she nodded before turning on her heels and walking away.

There was no line to enter the other bar, but bodies filled every inch of space in the room. The low ceilings made the club feel smaller than it probably was. Pictures of famous musicians hung on the pink stucco walls below a string of patio lights. The smell of sweat, cologne, and tequila permeated the air, and I tried my best to hold my breath. I walked straight to the bar and ordered myself a scotch.

As I leaned against the bar, I surveyed the room. Most people danced in the center, some gathered at tables shouting over the loud music, while others made out against the back wall. A particular couple caught my attention. The girl had long wavy brown hair, but I couldn't see her face because some man sucked at it while caressing her waist. For a moment, I thought it was Michaela, but a second glance confirmed my mistake. The thought of bending over her, kissing Michaela's lips, her hips pressed against me, made me groan and I turned back to the bar to take a swig from my drink. *Focus, Hunter.*

I prodded the room, looking for any familiar signs of a manticore—larger-than-normal frame for a male, tall for a female. Many of the people in this room displayed those attributes, but a deep inhale of their scent confirmed they were all human. *What was that?*

I caught the scent of something different. It could be a manticore but he was too far for me to be sure. I walked toward the back of the room where I first detected the smell and its potency grew. Yes, it definitely was a manticore, I was sure of it. When I looked around, I didn't see anyone that signaled my kind, but it didn't mean he wasn't here; he was simply good at hiding. My face must have shown my determination because as I moved toward the back of the room, people scampered out of my way. I relaxed my chest and took another deep breath, hoping to locate this manticore when the scent of sandalwood hit me and I took a step back. I closed my eyes as my heart raced and my blood heated.

Her scent had always affected me like this, like no one else's. It was her; Michaela was here. *Impossible!*

Michaela

The first two bars Nicholas and I hit were both duds. I had circled the room several times, holding my amulet and listening for a manticore's heartbeat, but there was none. The club two doors down from this one had a line up around the building, so we agreed to try it later when we hoped it would be less busy. This one was crowded but had no lineup.

"What can I get you, Michaela?" asked Nicholas as we maneuvered through the crowded room to get to the bar.

"I'm fine. I think I'm still buzzing from the drink at the last bar." For a moment, I was dizzy when I walked into this place and still felt a little uneasy. "You go ahead. I'll meet you over there," I said, and pointed to a corner near the back of the room. I walked past a couple kissing against the wall, averting my eyes to give them privacy, although I doubted they cared.

I closed my eyes and clasped my amulet as I leaned against the back wall. Music blared from the speakers to my left and people shouted all around me. I narrowed my focus to press these sounds into a tiny compartment in my mind and I squeezed them in there until the noise softened in my head.

I waited and listened for the sound of a manticore's heart. It came softly at first. I squeezed the background noise further away until the loudest sound in my mind was the rhythmic beating. *Ba-ba-boom.* There it was. That was it. I could hear it clearly now, louder than anything else in the club. *Ba-ba-boom ba-ba-boom.* Wait. There was an echo—no, not an echo, but a second heartbeat. There were two manticores in this club. But they were not together; one heartbeat was straight ahead, and the other was moving away from me.

I turned toward the moving target and followed the sound. My eyes were still closed, but I gently pulled at bodies in my way. "Hey, watch it," someone called out. I opened my eyes, but I could still hear the heartbeat, even though it was fainter now and the sound of the club came roaring back. I spotted a man push the back door open and leave into the indigo night. I didn't hesitate; I followed him.

Once outside, I found myself in an alleyway. Tall garbage bins lined the back walls and I couldn't see anything immediately to the left or right of me. I ran into the middle of the alley and checked right—nothing. I turned left and spotted a man walking with his hands in his pockets briskly near the end of the road. "Wait," I called out. He turned to look at me, but then immediately spun left into another street or alley. I couldn't be sure from this distance.

I raced after him, not knowing what I would say when I finally caught up to him, but knew I needed to find him. Before I could reach the spot where the manticore had turned, I heard footsteps behind me. They pounded against the pavement and my heart raced with fear. A manticore I could control, a strange man in an alley with a gun, I could not. The steps did not slow down, instead, they grew louder. Fight or flight? It took me only a moment to decide—I kicked off my heels and ran.

My heart hammered against my chest, the sound of my heartbeat now the only thing I could hear.

Please God, let me just get to the crowded front street.

I didn't make it. A hand grabbed my shoulder and spun me around. That same hand encircled my waist while his other hand grabbed the back of my head right before he pushed me against the hard stone wall. His hand cushioned the blow, but I still gasped and stared into a pair of familiar amber eyes. They looked livid.

"Michaela," he whispered harshly, right before his mouth slammed into mine. Recognizing Hunter didn't slow down my adrenaline at all—my heart raced and my body hummed at his touch. I kissed him back equally as hard and clawed at his back. I felt safe, relieved, and angry. I wanted to punish him for scaring me and judging the way he pushed his tongue through my lips, he wanted to punish me, too. Moving my hands behind him, I pulled his body closer to mine.

With a growl, he lifted me, and I wrapped my legs around his waist. He pushed my hair away from my neck and sucked at the spot just above my shoulder. I moaned; he knew what that spot did to me. I gripped the back of his neck and ran my fingers up his scalp, then back through his hair. He squeezed my thigh. I felt the urgency in his fingers when he moved his hand across my body. He pulled my panties to one side and placed his palm against my warm flesh. "You're wet," he said. I simply nodded, unable to speak at that moment.

He took his hand away with a moan and wrestled with the front of his pants. Then he was there, and I gasped at the pleasure of feeling him inside me. He moved us against the wall and rocked his body into mine. Dropping my head back against the stone, I panted, trying to keep up with his unwavering momentum. Normally, he was quite gentle, but this night, he took me without preamble or any softness. He was untamed and wild, and I hung on until the force of his movements pushed me to my limits. I fell hard and collapsed into his arms. He growled again but didn't stop. Instead, he carried on without allowing me a moment to catch my breath. I felt another rush building within me and cried out at the intensity of my second orgasm. Grasping my hips, Hunter threw his head back and roared out his own pleasure. I clung to him and he dropped his head forward, resting his forehead on my shoulder. He panted, harsh breaths overpowering my gasps for air. When I could finally breathe, I looked up and whispered, "*Hi.*"

His lips spread across my bare shoulder; I imagined them parting in a smile. The tip of his teeth grazed my flesh and it gave me goosebumps. Those teeth could kill another human. It was a good thing I was immune to his venom.

When he raised his head and stared into my eyes, his gaze finally softened. His eyes creased and his brow furrowed. "What are you doing here?"

"Same thing as you," I said with a smile. But then added more somberly, "I came to help you catch the killer."

He blew out a breath and slowly let me slide down until my legs touched the ground. I teetered, and he held me until I stood steadily on my own two feet.

"That was quite the greeting," I said as he took a moment to pull himself together.

He shook his head but smiled. Stepping toward me, he gathered me back into his arms. "When I saw you leave through the back door, I couldn't get there fast enough to stop you. I knew you would follow that manticore. I sensed him as well."

I had forgotten all about the other manticore. "Oh my gosh, Hunter. We lost him for sure by now."

"Yes, I'm afraid so, but I can't seem to regret it," he grinned.

"Hunter, this is serious. He can hurt someone tonight."

"I don't think he'll try anything. He knew someone was following him tonight. I don't think he'll risk it. You may have bought us another day to catch him."

I prayed Hunter was right and he wouldn't try hurting anyone.

"Are you by yourself?" Hunter asked.

"Oh, no! Nicholas!" I shouted and ran back toward the club. The door did not open from the outside, so I banged as hard as I could until someone finally opened it. Hunter held it for me as I ran inside and faced a wall of bodies. "Excuse me, excuse me, please," I said as I tried to squeeze past them. Nicholas stood at the corner I had pointed to earlier and I was so relieved to find him there.

"Michaela," he said when he spotted me. "Thank God. I worried when I didn't find you here. I hoped you had just gone to the bathroom or something." Or something was definitely the one.

"I kind of bumped into someone," I said and pointed behind me with my thumb. Nicholas's eyes looked over my shoulder and grew wider. I suspected he had just spotted Hunter.

"Oh boy," he said. "Is he angry?"

"He got over it," I answered, and held back a grin.

"Hello, Nicholas." Hunter nodded.

"Hi, Hunter." Nicholas gave a sheepish smile but otherwise stood his ground when Hunter frowned at him. "I would not abandon her when she asked for my help," Nicholas shouted over the loud music. "So don't give me that look."

Hunter reluctantly straightened his face, and if I had to guess, he appreciated that Nicholas had my back.

"Let's get out of here," I said, and led Hunter and Nicholas out of the club. When we got outside, I raised my hand to hail a cab, but Hunter stopped me.

"Wait," he said. "I need to do something before we leave." He pulled out his phone and began typing. I waited, knowing who he was texting.

When he finished, he put his phone down and looked at me. "Michaela, I came here with Vivienne. I am sorry I didn't tell you."

"Um, I'll just give you guys a minute," said Nicholas and walked away.

Turning back to Hunter, I said, "I know she's here." I crossed my arms, keeping my anger in check.

"You do? How?"

"Professor Wallace told me."

When his eyebrows pulled together and confusion marred his face, I waved it off. "I'll explain later. What I don't know is, why weren't you honest with me?" I smacked his chest and blew out a frustrated sigh. "I also don't know why we continue to have the same argument. You can't keep things from me, Hunter. Not for my protection, my own good, or any other reason you think you may have." I'd lost control of my arms, waving them around as I argued.

He ground his jaw and looked up in the air as though looking for the right words. "It isn't so simple for me, Michaela. My instincts are to protect you. But..."

I put my hand up to interrupt him, and he simply held it against his chest. "But I was wrong. I am learning, albeit slowly, but I am getting the hang of this no-secrets-between-us thing. Give me time. It's a lot for a manticore to learn."

I twisted my mouth but forgave him because he really did look sincere in his apology and I also felt a little guilty. "I'm sorry, too."

When he raised his eyebrow, I elaborated. "I didn't pick up the phone each time you called, even though I could have. I knew it would bug you and I wanted to punish you a little bit."

He shook his head, then pulled me into his arms. "You little minx," he growled into my ear.

A text binged on his phone, and he pulled it out of his pocket. "It's Vivienne. She says she's fine and progressing well with Alexander."

"Who's Alexander?" I asked.

"I can explain on the way. Your hotel room or mine?" He waggled his eyebrows at me. I shook my head. "Yours."

"Michaela, Hunter!" Nicholas called out from further down the sidewalk. He had hailed a cab while we were hashing things out.

"Go on, Nicholas. I'll head back to Hunter's hotel."

"Um... that's great," said Hunter. "But we still need a ride there."

He held my hand and walked us over to the street. “Thanks, Nicholas. We’ll share the cab with you.”

Nicholas took the front seat while Hunter and I climbed into the back.

Eight

Michaela

We were in Hunter's hotel room the next morning waiting for Vivienne. Hunter had brought me up to speed on the manticore family dynamics here in Oslo. He had also told me Vivienne had met with one of the family members last night at a club and would update us on her conversation with Alexander Larsen.

I had showered and blow-dried my hair and was making a cup of coffee when Hunter slid his arms around me. "You smell amazing," he whispered against my hair. I crossed my arms over his and tilted my head up to see him. He smiled, and I sighed, knowing I could never remain angry with him for very long. A knock interrupted me saying so. Hunter kissed my temple then walked away to open the door.

"Vivienne, come in." Hunter stepped back and Vivienne appeared with full makeup and hair flawlessly tousled, as though a team of stylists had just spent hours on it. I blew out a breath. I really had to get over Vivienne.

"Good morning, Vivienne," I said and put a smile behind it.

"Hello, Michaela." She smiled back, then glanced at Hunter.

"Go on. Whatever you have to say, you can say it in front of Michaela. No more secrets," he said. Hunter walked over to the small table and pulled out a chair for me and Vivienne before sitting down himself. "Did Alexander tell you anything of significance?"

Vivienne sat with her spine straight, then crossed her legs. "He knows you're here," she said. "He told me to tell you he also knows *why* you are here and that he had nothing to do with it."

Hunter leaned back in his chair. "That doesn't exactly convince me to check him off my list."

"Did he mention who he thinks *is* responsible for the attacks?" I asked.

Vivienne turned to me, then back to Hunter. "He said it was one of the Pedersens."

Hunter barked out a laugh. "Which one? Hans Pedersen? The head of the Pedersen family and wealthiest man in Norway? How convenient of him to point the finger at his nemesis."

"Actually, he mentioned his son Mathias. I asked him why and he simply replied, 'because the man is *gal*'."

"Gal?" I asked, unfamiliar with the word.

"It means crazy in Norwegian," explained Vivienne. "I don't know about Pedersen but I don't think Alexander or anyone in his family is responsible."

Hunter raised his eyebrow. "And why is that?"

"They've built an empire out of nothing. The attacks had no motive other than to attract attention and Alexander isn't looking for any setbacks. He has a clear plan to become the wealthiest man in Norway and perhaps beyond."

"Those attacks could be a warning to the Pedersens, a demonstration of power, something to signal a change in leadership," Hunter argued.

Vivienne shook her head. "I didn't get that impression. He seems focused on business, not power."

"Never underestimate a manticore's desire for power. It's always there."

Vivienne shook her head. "We need more information. We can't go around pointing fingers and accusing innocent people."

Hunter sighed, closed his eyes, and leaned back in his chair again.

An idea popped into my head. "What if we put out a reward?"

"A reward? For what?" Vivienne flicked her long hair back behind her shoulder.

"Someone must know something. If a manticore's desire for power is a dominant instinct, then let's use that to our benefit. Offer a reward to anyone that can provide information leading to the capture of this killer manticore."

"Money will not work. Most manticores have more money than they need," said Vivienne.

"Not money, power," I reminded her. "Offer a position on the King's Council. When is the last time he has ever given a foreigner such a role in the kingdom?"

"Never," replied Hunter, sitting forward again. "It's never happened and this could work." He stood up from the table and started pacing the room. "The position will allow the manticore to have the king's ear and be a part of major decisions in the kingdom. It's something we have never shared outside of the family." Hunter frowned. "I would have to speak to my father before we communicate this to the manticores in Norway."

"If your father is looking to modernize manticores, then this is one way to do it—turning the monarchy into a democracy," I said.

"I wouldn't go that far," said Hunter sardonically. "But I think opening a position up to outside members is an effective way to include the magistrates around the world."

"Keep your friends close..." I smirked.

"And your enemies closer," finished Vivienne.

I narrowed my eyes at her. "Exactly."

Looking between the both of us and sensing the sudden tension in the room, Hunter asked, "Vivienne, was there anything else Alexander said worth noting?"

Vivienne continued to hold my gaze. "He said something about

Hans's wife passing away last year. But nothing that would lead us to the attacker."

"All right. I will call my father now, then contact Astrid. She will relay the message to the manticores here in Norway. If someone knows something, they will talk. I'm sure of it."

Hunter grabbed his phone and moved closer to the window to make his call.

I wasn't finished with Vivienne, though. Leaning forward onto the table, I stared at her. "I don't know what you think is going on here, but your time with Hunter is over. He is married to me now."

Vivienne stared back. "I'm only here to help," she said, crossing her arms underneath her chest. "You have nothing to worry about. I see the way he looks at you. I don't think he ever looked at me that way."

I leaned back. "What do you mean?"

"He looks at you like you are the only one in the room. Like no one else exists if you are there. I don't excuse what I did, but if Hunter had given me an ounce of what he gives to you, I would never have strayed."

Surprised to hear the reason for their breakup but not wanting to give myself away, I held my composure. There was something in Vivienne's eyes that told me she still loved Hunter. Maybe she always would. I would just have to learn to deal with it.

"Do you want to fill me in on the complete Norwegian family history? See if perhaps there's anything we've missed? I can't stand waiting for something to happen. I have to keep busy."

Vivienne nodded and grabbed the notepad and pen next to the bed. She wrote the names of the two largest families and went down the family tree. She was about to tell me the story of how Pedersen's son was killed when Hunter interrupted us. "My father didn't hesitate. He thought it was a promising idea. So, I called Astrid, and she is spreading the word as we speak."

"That's great," I said, pleased at how quickly everything was progressing. "But what do we do now?"

"Since everyone knows we are in town, I think we should pay the Pedersens a visit. Ask them some questions and see how they respond."

"Good idea," I said and when Hunter took a deep breath, opening his mouth as though he were about to say something, I added, "Don't even think about leaving me behind."

He sighed. "Fine. But say nothing about being a Shed."

"I know. Professor Wallace already lectured me about it."

"Good. I trust the manticores in New York. They battled with you, fought by your side. I am not familiar with the Norwegian ones. I prefer not to find out they would sooner betray me than shake hands with you."

"What about Nicholas? He could probably go back home now."

"Who's Nicholas?" asked Vivienne.

"He's my mentor but more like my dad, really."

"I'll be happy to stay with him in Oslo while we wait for information."

"Uh, I don't know how comfortable he will feel around you, Vivienne. No offense, but the manticore thing makes him a little uneasy."

"Don't worry, Michaela. I'll take care of him for you. Don't I always take good care of the men in your life?"

Without thinking, I lunged for her, but Hunter held me back.

"Vivienne," he reprimanded.

"I'm sorry," she said, her hands in the air. "I just couldn't help it. She made it too easy." She chuckled and closed the door behind her.

"I don't like her," I said.

"You don't have to like her," Hunter soothed. "You just have to trust her."

"Do you trust her?"

Hunter paused, his mouth slightly opened, then he nodded. "Yes. She has no reason to hurt him."

I shook my head. "I'm calling Nicholas and warning him to be careful around her," I said, reaching for my phone in my purse.

"You don't have to do that," Hunter said, watching me. Then leaned down to kiss me.

I narrowed my eyes at him and dialed Nicholas's number, anyway.

Nine

Michaela

"That's Astrid," Hunter said when we stepped off the elevator. I followed his gaze to a woman wearing jeans, brown boots, and a felt hat.

"Were you expecting her?" I asked. He shook his head and continued walking toward her.

"Astrid, what are you doing here? Do you have any new information?" he asked.

She stared at me, then pursed her lips at Hunter. I smiled, realizing he hadn't introduced us yet and Astrid was an old-fashioned kind of manticore.

"My apologies. This is my wife, Michaela. Michaela, this is Astrid."

Astrid stuck out her arm and firmly shook my hand in hers. Once the formalities were out of the way, she looked past Hunter's shoulder, gazing at the bar where several hotel patrons sat and drank. "Some of my men have found an increased number of manticores hanging around this hotel lately," she said. "I came to check it out, just in case I noticed any new or suspicious faces that don't really belong in a hotel lobby at this time of day."

Hunter and I both looked around the lobby at the same time. Then Hunter raised his eyebrow and said, "And have you found anything suspicious?"

"I've noticed a couple of manticores hanging around. But they both had their reasons for being here."

"And those were?" Hunter prodded.

"One was meeting with a business associate while another was picking up a hotel guest. Both alibis checked out."

I breathed out a sigh of relief.

"But I'd still be careful if I were you. I have a bad feeling about this case."

"Me too, Astrid," said Hunter. "Me too."

"Let me know how it goes with the Pedersens tonight."

"We will," I said, calling out to her as we walked out the front doors.

Hunter drove us along the coast until he pulled up to a white stucco mansion with a black-tiled roof. The house backed onto a private pier and I could see a yacht parked in the back.

"Not too shabby for non-royalty," I said.

"They may not be manticore royalty, but they are one of the wealthiest families in Europe," Hunter said, stepping out of the car.

When he opened my car door, I asked, "They are expecting us, right?"

He smiled. "Yes. Astrid secured us an invitation for this evening."

I stepped out of the car. "I'm a little worried that something may happen at the bar scene tonight," I said.

Hunter reached for my hand and held it as we walked up the light grey interlocked pathway leading to the front door. He turned to me. "If I do not receive any leads by the end of dinner, we will scour the clubs tonight together. I don't want anyone else getting hurt either while we sit here and wait."

Hunter's plan sounded good to me, so I relaxed and prepared myself to greet the Pedersens. "Oh, do they speak English? I don't know any Norwegian words."

"They do," he chuckled. "You looked terrified for a moment."

"I was," I laughed, and he squeezed my hand as we approached the two large steel front doors. The home was very modern, surprising for such an old family.

Shortly after ringing the doorbell, a stout older woman answered the door.

"We are looking for Hans Pedersen?" Hunter said to the unsmiling woman.

"Hunter Durand?" A man called from the hallway. He wore light grey slacks and a crisp white shirt. He had sandy blond hair and amber eyes with creases around them, the kind you get from smiling too much. He was tall and muscular and quite attractive, made more so by his high spirits.

"I'm William Pedersen. My father will be joining us shortly along with my brother Mathias."

He walked over and extended his hand in greeting. Hunter shook it, then placed his hand on my shoulder. "This is my wife, Michaela."

I reached forward to shake William's hand, and he returned it with great enthusiasm. His cheerful demeanor was inviting, and I found the knots at my shoulders, which I hadn't realized were there, loosening, and I happily returned his jovial greeting.

A woman with short dark hair similar in height to my five-foot-four frame joined us in the hallway. William noticed her arrival. "Anne, dear. Come meet the Durand family. This is Hunter Durand and his wife, Michaela." The woman hastened her step and smiled demurely when she reached us.

"Pleased to meet you," said Hunter.

"The honor is mine," replied Anne. She blushed when they shook hands, and her grip was barely there when she accepted mine. Her reserved smile appeared genuine, though.

"You must excuse my wife," chuckled William. "She was a little overwhelmed when I told her the heir of the Manticore Kingdom and his wife would be joining us for dinner."

Anne's blush deepened, stretching from her hairline down to the white blouse she wore. This only made William chuckle again, but he pulled his wife into his arms as though he could transfer his good humor to her. She smiled, but it looked more like a grimace. When William finally let her go and asked us to follow him down the hallway, I hung back to speak to Anne.

"Thank you for accommodating us at the last minute. We truly appreciate it."

"It is my pleasure, Ms. Durand," she said, staring straight ahead, her hands clasped in front of her.

"Please, call me Michaela."

"Michaela," she said and smiled softly when she turned to look at me. "I hope you are enjoying your time in Norway."

"It's beautiful here," I told her. "Have you lived in Norway your whole life?"

"Yes, but I have visited many places."

"I hope to travel more once my daughter gets older," I said.

"You have a daughter? With Hunter?"

A feeling of protectiveness came over me, and for a moment, I wanted to take it back. I wanted to keep Violet away from manticores we did not know well. So, I simply said, "Yes." And mentally warned myself to keep her out of future conversations, even though Anne seemed pleasant enough.

"William and I have two children."

"Will they be joining us for dinner?"

"No, they are older and living abroad. One is in France and another in Belgium."

I turned slightly to peek at Anne. She looked to be around my age, but with her manticore genes, she could be well into her sixties and still look twenty-seven.

We followed Hunter and William into the dining room and I was about to take my seat when I thought it best to give my grandmother a call so I could speak to Violet before she went to bed. I knew it would be too late by the time we finished dinner and mentioning Violet a few minutes ago made me miss her like crazy. I turned to Anne. "Could you tell me where I would find the bathroom? I'd like to wash my hands before dinner."

"Of course," said Anne, and turned to exit the dining room.

I glanced back at Hunter, his brow furrowed with a question in his eyes, and I smiled. "I'll only be a minute." He nodded but watched me as I joined Anne in the hallway.

"Take this corridor all the way to the end and then turn right. The powder room will be the first door on your left."

"Thank you," I said and rushed my steps until I reached the end of the hallway and turned right. The powder room door was open, so I quickly went inside and shut the door behind me. I pulled out my cell and dialed my house number. My grandmother picked up the phone after the third ring.

"Hello?"

"*Nonna*? It's Michaela. How's everything?"

"*Tutto bene*. Everything is fine, *bella*. Violet just fell asleep. How are you?"

"Oh," I said, disappointed I had missed her. "I was hoping to hear her voice. Hold on a second. I'll try again with a video call so I can watch her sleep."

She chuckled. "She is resting. Stop worrying."

I wanted to argue that I wasn't worrying. I just wanted to see her, but maybe she was right. I should relax knowing Violet was safe, sleeping in her bed.

"How is the search going in Norway?" she asked.

"Well, I found Hunter, but we haven't found the killer yet. I hope we can solve this soon before someone else gets hurt."

"You will, Michaela. I have faith in you."

"Thank you, *Nonna.* I should get back to dinner. Kiss Violet for me when she wakes up."

"I will, *bella,* and don't you worry about *Violetta.* I will take good care of her."

A lump formed in my throat. "Thank you," I whispered.

"Good night, Michaela."

"Good night, *Nonna.*"

I ended the call and washed my hands before heading out of the powder room. I was still thinking of Violet when I stepped out and didn't notice the other person until I slammed into him. *Oof.*

A pair of large hands caught my shoulders. His fingers pressed into my flesh and something flashed in his amber eyes before he let me go. I had to take a step back to steady myself. His eyes bore into mine and his brow creased.

"Who the hell are you?" he asked in a cold voice.

"I'm so sorry I ran into you. I wasn't paying attention." His face still looked angry, so I introduced myself.

"I'm Michaela Durand," I said, and offered him a smile.

He didn't smile back. Instead, he raised his eyebrow. "You're Hunter's wife?"

"Yes," I sighed in relief. At least now he knew I wasn't some sort of intruder.

"You're not a manticore," he said and crossed his arms.

Perhaps that was the reason he stared into my eyes earlier. They were not amber or gold-rimmed, but purple. I shook my head, "No, but I see that you clearly are."

It wasn't just his eyes that gave him away, but the way he could intimidate me. Predators always felt in control in front of their prey. Only this predator didn't know that I wasn't entirely human. He had long sandy blond hair, which he kept tied back, and wore dark jeans and a black high-neck sweater. He looked to be around Hunter's age, maybe younger. It was hard to guess with manticores. I suddenly realized who he was.

"Mathias?" I asked.

A smile crept upon his face. "I see you've heard of me."

Cocky bastard, wasn't he?

"Your brother mentioned you would be joining us for dinner," I informed him.

"I see," he said and continued to stare at me.

I felt uncomfortable under his scrutiny and decided it was time to move along. "We should head back. They must be waiting for us to start dinner."

He waved his hand forward and said, "After you, Ms. Durand."

I pivoted on my heel and walked down the hallway. Mathias didn't bother to catch up, so I felt his eyes on me as I walked across the tiled foyer. My heels clicked on the porcelain, but he made no noise. A chill ran down my spine and the instinct to fight or flight ran through me again. I shook it off, reminding myself he was not out to get me. I sighed a breath of relief, nonetheless, when I reached the dining room and met with a familiar pair of warm amber eyes. Hunter smiled, but it faltered when he noticed my face. I quickly fixed it with a smile of my own and headed to sit next to him. William sat across from Hunter, his wife to his left, leaving a seat directly in front of me for Mathias. I groaned inwardly, realizing I would have to sit across from him for most of the evening.

"Oh good, I see you've met Mathias," William clasped his hands in front of him, then pointed to Hunter. "May I present to you my brother Mathias? Mathias, it is my honor to present the heir, Hunter Durand." Hunter stood and shook Mathias's hand.

"This is my wife, Michaela," Hunter said, pointing to me as he sat back down.

"Yes, we've met," I murmured at the same time Mathias said, "Yes, she assaulted me in the corridor earlier."

Hunter turned to look at me and my eyes grew larger. I couldn't believe he had said that. "I did not assault you," I hissed, perhaps a little too loudly.

Mathias smiled, but it did not reach his eyes. "I was only kidding. We merely bumped into each other."

"Thank you," I said.

"I take it you didn't capture Hunter's heart with your sense of humor," Mathias replied, his voice laced with sarcasm. He reached for the bottle of wine in front of him and poured himself a glass.

I narrowed my eyes at him but kept my mouth shut. He would not bate me into making a scene.

"Is something the matter?" asked Hunter, looking at me, then Mathias.

"Not at all," I said, adjusting my napkin on my lap. "Some people just bruise a lot more easily than others." *And sometimes worse when it's their ego that takes a hit.* This guy had a chip on his shoulder and I didn't know why. I planned to ignore him for the rest of the night.

"Excuse my tardiness," a booming voice rang from the doorway. A tall, lean man with salt and pepper hair entered the room. His eyes met mine, and he walked toward us. Hunter stood, blocking the man from reaching me first.

"Hans Pedersen, I presume," Hunter said.

A small smile played on the man's lips, reminding me of William. "You presume correctly. I cannot tell you how pleased I am to have you and your lovely wife here with us for dinner. Please sit," he said, gesturing to the chair. Hunter and I lowered ourselves back into our seats and Hans Pedersen sat at the head of the table.

"It's disappointing we've never had the fortune of meeting sooner. Although, your father and I have had the pleasure of getting to know each other over the years." He clapped his hands together. "But we can rectify that starting tonight." His hearty laugh put everyone at ease, and I turned to Anne and smiled, avoiding Mathias. I didn't want to ruin the moment.

Hans joining us must have been the signal the servers needed to begin the meal. Three men wearing white jackets and gloves entered the room holding steaming porcelain bowls. A server set a bowl of seafood soup in front of me and the flavorful aroma warmed my chest. My stomach rumbled in anticipation.

"Bon appétit," announced Hans before digging in.

I brought the spoon to my lips, and the warm broth did not disappoint. But when the server came around with a sheep's head for the next course, I nearly tossed up the soup. Fortunately, he also offered other morsels, and I settled for the rack of lamb instead.

Polite conversation hummed throughout the meal and I was just about to take a bite of the chocolate cake when Mathias asked, "So how does a manticore marry a human without breaking any of the kingdom rules?"

He had his hands clasped in front of his face, staring at Hunter, as though he were seriously pondering this question rather than making an accusation.

"Hunter never told me what he was," I said, rushing to his defense.

"Maybe not, but you clearly know now," continued Mathias.

Hunter cleared his throat. "It was not easy, but no rules were broken and the king realized that Michaela was quite special." He smiled, but it didn't look right.

"Special?" asked Mathias. "But she's only human, correct?"

Hunter put down his spoon, and I put my hand on his thigh when I sensed the tension radiate from his body. The muscle underneath my fingers tensed.

"I understand you've never been to the kingdom, Mathias, so I will excuse your impertinence this time. But the king does not make any decision without taking the past and future into consideration.

He welcomed Michaela into our kingdom with open arms. Now, I suggest you eat your dessert before I lose my patience with you." Hunter stared back at Mathias, then picked up his spoon again.

"You must excuse my son," said Hans in a serious tone. "My wife and I did a poor job raising them after Erik died."

"Ah, father," said William, placing his hand over his father's and squeezing it. "Don't say that."

"Who's Erik?" I asked and immediately regretted it.

"He was my eldest," responded Hans, looking at me. "He was killed ten years ago."

I shivered at his words. "I'm so sorry," I whispered.

He smiled weakly. "When Mrs. Pedersen was pregnant with William, she was sure she'd lose the child."

Hunter turned to me. "You may not know this, Michaela, but having three children is uncommon for manticores. We do not sire children as easily as humans do."

"When William proved to be a healthy baby and then young boy," continued Hans. "My wife admitted we were one of the rare but lucky manticore families. Until our eldest son, Erik disappeared. It devastated her. She believed our family cursed and that she must pay back her blessing of three children. She threw herself into charity work, throwing fundraisers, galas, and starting foundations."

"It's all right, father," said William. "The work mother started is commendable. Anne and I, we're honored to continue her legacy."

A large lump formed in my throat and my eyes watered. The story broke my heart, and I didn't know what to say. Unfortunately, Mathias broke the silence.

"Have you come to Norway to track down the rogue?" asked Mathias, and I couldn't help but roll my eyes at his awful timing.

Hunter put down his spoon but remained calm. "Yes," he said and brought his elbows onto the table and folded his hands. "There have been two violent attacks in Norway that resemble the work of a manticore. We are here to make sure another attack does not happen."

"What makes you think it was a manticore and not just some violent human?" asked Mathias.

"Let's just say we are confident in our assumption," Hunter replied.

"Astrid told us about the reward," continued Mathias.

"Yes. I heard she is contacting all the manticores in the area. We want to catch him tonight if possible. Can you tell me where you were Mathias last night?"

"Me?" asked Mathias, a smile finally forming on his face, but he did not look happy. "You think I had something to do with this?"

"Surely, Hunter was not trying to accuse you, Mathias," said William. "He simply inquired if you've seen anything. Isn't that right?" William turned to Hunter, but Hunter continued to stare at Mathias.

"I was at home. The club scene does not interest me," replied Mathias.

"Well, there you have it," said William, trying to lighten the mood. Anne brushed her hair away from her face, frown lines marking her delicate features.

"You don't have to worry about Mathias," Hans said. "But I hope you catch this manticore before anyone else gets hurt."

I stared at Mathias, but he only had eyes for his father.

I hoped we caught him soon too.

Dinner ended shortly afterward with no incident. Walking back to the car, I felt relieved to be away from Mathias. The way he looked at me gave me hives.

"So, what did you think?" I asked Hunter when we were in the car.

"I think Mathias knows something."

I nodded, having suspected the same. "Now what?"

"I'm going to visit Alexander Larsen tonight. See if I get the same feeling from him."

I shivered. If Alexander Larsen were as creepy as Mathias, I'd prefer to stay back at the hotel.

Ten

Hunter

Just like the first time I was here, club-goers swarmed *Lexi's* front door wanting to get inside the nightclub. Owned by one of the most powerful, if not the richest, men in Norway was quite the attraction, it seemed. I'd asked Vivienne to contact Alexander to let him know I was on my way to see him. It took little convincing to get Michaela to stay behind. She mentioned going over some new reports from Olivia with Nicholas. She agreed to stay back with him to look it over.

Bypassing the lineup, I gave the bouncer at the door my name.

"Mr. Larsen is waiting for you at his private table downstairs," said the bouncer.

He led me through the crowded entrance and into the club, leaving an associate to handle the door. A blue tint flooded the room, and a techno beat pumped from the speakers. Sweat mixed with perfume saturated the air, but no one seemed to mind. People danced and laughed as I went in search of a killer.

The bouncer brought me to a table near the back. A winding staircase only a few feet away, most likely leading to a private second floor. A tall, blond Viking of a man, or as I knew better, a manticore, sat at a table with three women surrounding him. The women hung on his arms like leaves on a tree clinging to life. When I approached the table, he shook them off, and they scattered away toward the bar. He turned to watch them go and I noticed a scratch on the side of Alexander's face. Astrid had mentioned the victim had cut the killer.

Alexander Larsen stood when I approached the table and leaned forward with his hand extended. I cautiously shook it. "A pleasure to see royalty here in these parts," he said.

"From what I've heard, I understand you're the bigger name around here." I took a seat in a chair across the table from him. My back was to the dance floor, but Alexander was the only other predator in the room. My instincts detected no other manticore.

His lips curled, and he stretched his arms across the bench behind him, straining the buttons on his black shirt. "I guess that depends on who you ask. The fact that I am sitting in front of the Manticore Kingdom heir is quite the coup and a fortunate circumstance for me."

I watched Alexander as he spoke and couldn't help but stare at the mark on his face. He must have felt my eyes on the spot because he rubbed a finger across his cheek and smiled. "Someone got a little too excited from my attention the other night. I don't mind though; it was worth the nick."

I raised my gaze to look him in the eye, but he gave nothing away, nor did he seem uncomfortable by my silence.

"Where were you last night?" I finally asked.

"Why, what happened last night?" he drawled.

"Answer me," I snarled. My patience, after handling Mathias, teetered on the edge of a knife.

The smile fell from Alexander's lips. "I was with Vivienne all night."

"Vivienne Barros," I confirmed.

"The one and only," he grinned.

I hadn't spoken to Vivienne yet. Alexander might be telling me the truth. But why didn't Vivienne mention the mark on his face? I considered calling her at that moment, but if Vivienne were Alexander's alibi, would she give him up so easily? Perhaps Michaela was right. Could I trust Vivienne again? She had, after all, betrayed me in the most intimate way. Frustration tested my patience further, and I had little left for the man in front of me.

"Two people are already dead. If you know something about this killer manticore, tell me now."

"I have my suspicions," said Alexander, taking a sip of his drink, unflustered by my outburst.

A growl rumbled in my chest, but I didn't want to give Alexander the satisfaction that he was getting to me. Judging by the smirk on his face, however, I knew he had heard it.

He grinned wider and put his drink down. "The way I see it, there are two possibilities. One, we have a crazy manticore on the loose in Norway. Someone with no inhibitions nor regard for his own life or others. If that's true, this manticore must be a vagrant because my family and I have lived in these parts for centuries and someone that crazy doesn't stay quiet for very long. I would have heard about him by now."

"And the other possibility?" I raised my eyebrow.

"Someone who's been meticulously planning this with the resources not to get caught." Alexander looked past me toward the exit of the club. "I agreed to see you here tonight because I don't trust those Pedersens."

"Why not?"

"You probably don't know this, but our families were in business together once."

I raised my eyebrows because it was the first time I'd heard this. "Go on."

"Well, after Pedersen's son died, Hans was never the same man again. It wasn't very good for business."

"You really have a heart of stone, don't you?"

"Perhaps. But it hasn't steered me wrong yet."

"So you ended your business with him?"

"His wife ended it. She wanted to focus on charity work and, well, I did not." He took a sip of his drink. "Besides, his son Mathias and I never got on. He always stuck his nose where it didn't belong."

"And you make all the decisions for your family?"

"I do. My uncle Glen is the mayor, and he handles all government business. And me, well, I handle all the fun stuff. It works well. I've come to realize that partnership doesn't really suit me. I prefer to lead."

I'm sure you do.

"Which one do you think did it?" I asked.

"If you're asking me," said Alexander. "I'd say it was Mathias."

"Are you getting rid of the competition by accusing the Pedersens of murders they did not commit?"

Alexander simply smiled.

"What motive would Mathias have, anyway?" I prodded.

"I don't know. Maybe he likes to kill people because he's a narcissistic twat just like his brother Erik."

I shook my head. "Why would you say that about Erik? What can you tell me about him?"

"Erik was a pain in everyone's ass. He condemned the rules placed on manticores by the kingdom. He wanted to hunt, fight, and do whatever his instincts told him to do with no condemnation. Well, Astrid gave Hans one week to get his son under control before she took matters into her own hands with the help of the kingdom. Shortly afterward, Erik disappeared."

"What happened to him?" I asked, trying to remember if I'd heard of Erik Pedersen before this trip.

Alexander shook his head and brought his arms down from the bench to place them on the table. "No one knows for sure," he said, leaning forward. "Some think a bear attacked him. Others believe Astrid took him down."

"Astrid?"

"It's just talk. I don't think it was her. The old girl is just itching to use that spear though." Alexander chuckled.

My hands shook in frustration. Alexander had pointed his finger at several different manticores. Was it his way to detract attention from himself? My head spun, and I didn't trust the manticore in front of me.

"Other than conspiracy theories, do you have any evidence pointing to Mathias?"

"If I did, I'd tell you. I want that reward," confessed Alexander. "But I have nothing so far."

I stood from the table. "If you find something useful, call me." I had written my cell phone number on a notepad at the hotel earlier. I passed it along to him now.

He picked up the piece of paper and examined it. "I will certainly do that."

I turned and walked out of the club.

When I reached outside, a voice hissed from behind me. "What did Larsen have to say?" Turning, I faced Mathias and William.

"What are you two doing here?" I asked them.

William wrung his hands. "Michaela left her scarf at the house and my brother was adamant that we return it in person. We followed you back to your hotel, but then saw you leave again. Mathias thought it best to wait for you when we saw you go into *Lexi's*. Larsen doesn't have the best reputation."

"You came all the way here to check on me?" I asked, tilting my head and watching William's reaction.

"Yes. You're the heir to our kingdom and I'd feel responsible if something happened to you." William's eyes softened and he offered a weak smile in return.

I narrowed my eyes at Mathias, but he offered no further explanation.

"What did Larsen have to say?" he asked instead.

"He told me to be suspicious of your family," I replied.

Mathias scoffed. "Well, of course, he'd say that." He shoved his fists into his coat pockets. "You don't believe him, do you?"

"Not really," I said, walking up to my car. William and Mathias trailed behind me. If I could rule the Pedersens out, I could focus on Alexander Larsen. "But I'd like you both to stay inside the mansion for the next few days until everything settles." I directed the request to William.

He nodded, and I opened my car door. "Of course," he said.

But Mathias growled softly behind me as I walked away, raising tiny hairs behind my neck.

Eleven

Michaela

White sheets of paper covered the hotel room floor. Olivia had sent us the police chief's twenty-year case history after I'd requested it. I'd a hunch there was something in those files that would lead us to the killer manticore.

"The chief certainly kept himself busy," said Vivienne, using a perfectly manicured red fingernail to flip through her stack of papers. "He wrote several of the reports himself, instead of getting a junior to do it."

I didn't respond, too busy reviewing my own stack.

"Michaela, we've been at this for hours. There's nothing here," said Vivienne, sighing dramatically. I ignored her.

"Vivienne's right," Nicholas said in a muffled voice. He was more difficult to dismiss.

We needed a smoking gun, something that pointed us to the killer. "Hand me the police report from the night of the first murder five days ago," I said to Nicholas.

Nicholas stood to search for the sheet in a stack of papers next to the bed. "Here it is," he said and passed it to me.

I scanned it for the tenth time. I willed something to jump out at me, something I hadn't seen before. But nothing did. I closed my eyes and when I opened them they landed on a name. Sylvie Dunn. She had reported the police chief missing the night of his murder.

I picked up my phone and called Olivia.

"Hey Michaela, what can I do for you?" Olivia always got down to business. I appreciated it.

"Can you look someone up for me? She lives in Oslo and her name is Sylvie Dunn."

"Sure. Give me a minute," she said. Loud clicking on a keyboard was the only sound on the other end of the line. "I found her. Except, she goes not only by Sylvie Dunn."

"Really? That's what it says on the police report."

"Yeah, that is her official name. Unofficially, she's also known as Lady Sylvia."

"Lady Sylvia," I repeated. "Is she a Countess or something like that?"

"No. She's a stripper."

"Oh," I said and looked up at Vivienne and Nicholas.

"Well, is she?" asked Nicholas.

Vivienne shook her head, "Never heard of her, if she is," she murmured.

"Here's where she works," Olivia said. As she relayed the address, I grabbed a piece of paper beside me to jot it down.

"Thanks, Olivia."

"Anytime."

"So, are we going to another club?" asked Vivienne, putting down her stack of papers. Her eyes were hopeful.

"Um, sort of," I said, looking at my oversized sweater and tights. "But I think I need to change first."

Vivienne stood, stretching her long limbs and tousling her hair. "You're fine. Let's just get out of this hotel room already."

"Fine," I said. "But first, let me text Hunter and let him know where we're going." I quickly typed Hunter a message with the address. "Okay, let's go." I grabbed my jacket and closed the door behind us.

Nicholas immediately hailed a cab outside our hotel and we reached the club in less than twenty minutes.

"I must confess, I've never been to a bar like this before," said Nicholas as we walked toward the stainless-steel doors.

"Don't worry, Nicholas," said Vivienne with a grin. "We'll go easy on you for your first time."

"Don't be crude," I shot back.

Vivienne smirked and opened the door for Nicholas and me. I may have been a little nervous since it was my first time at such a place as well. I'd gone to bachelorette parties at clubs where men stripped, but I'd never been to one where women were the entertainers.

A man stood at the entryway. He nodded at Vivienne, but then stuck his hand out to Nicholas. "Ninety Krones," he said.

Nicholas reached into his wallet and pulled out a bill.

"Ninety dollars is the entry fee," I hissed.

"That's Krones. It's about ten US dollars."

"Oh," I said, settling back down.

The dark walls and corridor swallowed me whole in my black sweater, tights, and sneakers. Vivienne, as usual, stood out in a white fitted top, skinny jeans, and black high heels. She was like a beacon walking into the carpeted main room. A red hue painted the large room, and a hazy cloud of smoke lingered in the air. Small round tables and chairs littered the floor while waitresses wearing short shorts and barely-there crop tops weaved between the tables to the bar. Black walls, black carpet, black tables. Everything about this place blended together. The effect was intentional, I realized. It forced everyone's attention to the main stage, where a single spotlight shone on an empty stage.

"Where would we find Sylvie?" I asked.

Nicholas and Vivienne scanned the room. Vivienne's gaze landed near the back, next to the stage. "Michaela, you come with me. Nicholas, stay here and wait for Hunter."

Nicholas cleared his throat and took a seat near the bar. "I hope he arrives soon. This is a little awkward."

I squeezed Nicholas's shoulder, then rushed off to follow Vivienne as she approached a black door with a brass knob.

"Where are we going?" I asked when I caught up to her.

"I think this leads backstage."

It did, but a large man with boulders as biceps met us at the door. "Can I help you, ladies?"

I stuttered, but Vivienne calmly raised her purse. "Sylvie called me. She forgot something." The rock of a man eyed Vivienne, nodding his head, but narrowed his eyes when he looked at me.

"She's with me," said Vivienne.

"If you say so," he grunted and waved us both forward.

"Quick thinking," I said when we were out of earshot. "Now to find Sylvie."

"Lady Sylvia," Vivienne called out when we reached the main room in the back. The space was well lit with women half-dressed but fully made up, walking between clothing racks.

A woman with vibrant red hair turned around. She looked to be in her thirties, judging by the fine lines around her eyes. Although a hard life could have also contributed. Her toned body glistened in a dominatrix outfit—she carried a whip and all. It looked pretty hot, actually.

"That's me. Who wants to know?" asked Sylvie, one hand on her hip.

"Hi, I'm Michaela," I said, walking up to her. "I want to ask you some questions about a missing person's report you filed a few days ago."

Sylvie's face tightened, her cheeks hollowing as though she bit them from the inside. "He's not missing anymore and I don't want to talk about it." She turned and cracked her whip beside her. Vivienne and I both flinched, but Vivienne stepped forward. I stopped her with a hand on her shoulder.

"Let me handle it."

She waved me forward, "All yours."

"Sylvie. We know what happened to your friend and we want to help find the person responsible for hurting him, but we need your help to do it."

"What if I talk and he comes after me?" she asked, her back still to me.

I hesitated, not sure how to respond.

"We'll handle it before it gets to that," said Vivienne from behind me.

Sylvie turned around and stared at Vivienne. Her features hadn't softened, and I wasn't sure if she would talk or not.

"Sylvie!" shouted a man from behind the curtain. "You're on!"

Sylvie shrugged her shoulders and turned to leave.

"Wait," said Vivienne. "We're not done here. I just need two minutes."

"Well, unless your girl here wants to go on stage for me, I've got to go."

I laughed, but Vivienne's hard stare stopped me. "She's joking," I said, pointing to Sylvie.

"Actually, I wasn't."

"Just stall for two minutes," said Vivienne. "Take off your top or something. You're wearing a bra, right?"

"I'm not taking off my top," I hissed at her.

"Fine. Sing a song. Do whatever you need to do to stall them for a few minutes."

Vivienne pushed me forward toward the stage. I stumbled but walked up to the curtain.

"Who the hell are you?" whispered the man on stage.

"Um, I'm Lady Sylvia's opening act," I said, my hands shaking.

He stared at my clothes. "All right. Good luck out there." He turned to return to the stage but swiveled back. "What's your name?"

"M—" I paused. "Miki"

"Gentleman," he began once he returned on stage. "We have a special guest here with us tonight. Put your hands together for Miki."

At the sound of the applause, I pulled back the curtain and walked onto the stage.

Twelve

Hunter

I had received Michaela's message late, having already arrived at the hotel. But after plugging the address into my GPS, I reversed out of the hotel driveway and returned to the road. The location wasn't too far from where we stayed. I parked the car out front and stared up at the neon sign that read: At Your Pleasure. *What are they doing here?*

Having paid the entrance fee, I strode into the club. The scent of cigarettes nearly choked me, and I coughed to get the debris out of my lungs. The bar was situated to the left as soon as I walked into the main room. Small tables littered the black carpet between the bar at the front and the stage at the back. I stood at the bar looking for Michaela. There were several women with dark, curly hair, but none of them was her.

"Can I help you, handsome?" A buxom blonde carrying a round black tray with a couple of drinks on it stopped in front of me. Her red lips curved up into a smile.

"Perhaps," I said. "I'm looking for a woman with brown curly hair, this tall." I raised my hand to my upper chest.

The woman tilted her head and smacked her gum. "I'll dye my hair brown if that's what you're into."

"I'm flattered, but that won't be necessary." I spotted a head of salt and pepper hair and recognized Nicholas immediately. "Thank you, but I think I found her."

Nicholas was facing the stage but his hand also cupped his eyes, averting his gaze from the naked woman gliding down a pole.

I fixed my smile and sat in front of him, my back to the stage, blocking his view.

"Thank you," he said with a sigh and dropped his hand onto the table.

"You know the point of this establishment is to watch the entertainment."

"Yes, well, there's quite an eyeful to see. In my day, shoulders were enough to make a man's head spin."

"I remember a time when a woman's ankle was enough for me," I said, but I digressed. "What are we doing here, anyway?" I asked. Then looking around the room, "And where the heck is Michaela?"

"Michaela found a lead. A woman who first reported the police chief missing. She went around back with Vivienne, I—"

Nicholas's gaze lifted above my head and his eyes rounded as big as saucers.

"Nicholas—" I turned around to see what startled him and that's when I saw her. Michaela stood on the stage, thankfully fully dressed, hand raised, shielding her eyes from the spotlight. "What the f—" I stood up to grab her, but Nicholas pulled me down. "Maybe this is part of their plan."

"What plan?" I asked in disbelief.

"I don't know, but just give her a minute."

A song I didn't recognize came on. There were no words, but a sultry saxophone wailed from the speakers. Michaela swayed awkwardly to the music. Her left hand reached for the pole. She brought her right hand down, away from her face, and ran it along the side of her body. A man whistled beside me. A growl rumbled in my chest. Encouraged by the whistle, she wrapped one leg around the pole while her left hand still held on tightly. She swung around once.

Her long hair lifted off her shoulders and fell seductively across her face. *Where the hell did she learn to do that?*

She swayed to the music again. This time she didn't look awkward at all. She looked seductive. Her eyes were closed, and she seemed lost in the moment.

With both hands, she lifted her hair off her neck, letting it fall slowly through her fingers. Gyrating her hips, she squatted down low, then popped back up again. My body stiffened.

No, no, no. This show is over.

A loud growl erupted from my lips, and I stood up from the table staring at her. Michaela's eyes landed on me, and I froze. Caught in her gaze, she smiled and lifted her sweater just high enough to reveal her navel. The move was sexy as hell and I would've appreciated it more if the guy next to me hadn't shouted, "Take it off, sweetheart."

No fucking way.

I jumped on stage in one fluid motion, lifted Michaela up and over my shoulder.

"Hunter," she laughed and pounded on my back. "Put me down."

"Not until we're off this stage," I shouted back.

I pulled back the curtain and set her down on the other side. "What the hell were you thinking?" I asked, waving my hand toward the stage.

Despite my obvious anger, she smiled. "It was kind of fun."

"Fun?" My eyes nearly popped out of my face.

"Yeah, watching you watch me."

"Michaela, there were a dozen other men out there as well."

"Yes, but I only had eyes for you," she said. She had no idea how those words affected me. I pushed her against the wall and breathed in her scent. Overwhelmed by the smell of her, I set my lips on her neck and sucked at her sweet spot.

She wrapped her leg across my hip, and I pulled her in closer, grinding myself against her.

She moaned and I caught her lips with mine. Every time I kissed her, I lost all sense of my surroundings. Otherwise, I would have heard the man before he pulled me away.

"You can't be back here," he shouted.

The anger in my eyes must have been clear because he took a step back from me.

"It's all right," said Michaela. "We were leaving." She pulled me down a hallway.

She flung her arms around my neck, and instinctively I pulled her up against me. My body hadn't forgotten what she'd done on that stage and wanted satisfaction. I led her toward a darkened corner when a voice stopped me. "Hunter!" It was Vivienne, and I tried to ignore her.

"Hunter, stop. Vivienne's calling you," Michaela said, dropping her arms from my neck.

"I know. I plan to ignore her until I'm finished with you."

Michaela laughed but dug in her heels. She pulled me back toward the bright room, away from our private corner. I sighed but walked back with her toward Vivienne. A woman wearing a black leather bra and skirt, holding a whip, walked past us and onto the stage.

"Did Sylvie tell you anything?" Michaela asked.

"She told me she reported her boyfriend, the former police chief, missing when he didn't return from a meeting with the mayor."

"Isn't the mayor Glen Larsen?" I asked.

"He is," said Vivienne. "But she also said that her boyfriend had complained about a nasty phone call he'd received the day before. He said the caller blasted him for having done a poor job of following up on cases, one in particular."

"Which one?" I asked.

"The Erik Pedersen case."

"Who was the caller?" I had a feeling this was the lead we needed.

Vivienne smirked. "Mathias Pedersen."

Mathias again.

"I think I need to pay Mathias another visit," I said. "Michaela, are you coming? I'm not leaving you alone this time."

"I wasn't alone," she mumbled, then turned to Vivienne. "Can you take Nicholas back to the hotel for me?"

"Yes, of course," said Vivienne. "Just keep me posted."

"I will," Michaela shouted back and followed me out of the club.

The chilly night air blasted across my face, and Michaela visibly shivered next to me. I took off my coat and wrapped it around her shoulders. "Wait here. I'll run and bring the car to pick you up."

She nodded and clutched my coat at her neck. "Hurry," she said.

I took off in a sprint and reached my car in just a few minutes. As promised, I turned the heat to max and drove toward the back of the club where I'd left Michaela. She stood dancing on the spot, her movements making me smile until a shadow crept up beside her. I couldn't see the figure, but his shape was visible in the lamplight, and he held something in his hand.

"Michaela!" I shouted and honked my horn. Michaela jumped back and swung her head from side to side. I pulled up beside her and ran out of the car toward the shadow. But there was no one there. *Had I imagined it, or was someone following her?*

"What was it?" she asked when I joined her in the car.

"I thought I saw something, but I guess it was nothing."

"What did you see?"

I shook my head. "Just a shadow. It was probably someone walking to their car."

She nodded and rubbed her hands in front of the vent. I put the incident out of my mind and headed for the Pedersen mansion.

When we arrived, I nearly ran to the door, Michaela easily keeping up with me, and pounded with perhaps a little too much force.

The shadow at the back of the club had me spooked, and I wanted to catch this killer as soon as possible.

The same older woman as before answered, but this time, she bid me to come in. "Is Mathias at home?" I asked her.

"He is, sir. I'll fetch him."

"Thank you," I said and paced the foyer.

"Hunter," Michaela said. "You're making me nervous. What's gotten into you?"

I stopped and reached for her hand. "I'm sorry. I just have this feeling that something is not right."

"Hunter, what a surprise to see you again so soon," Mathias said, striding toward us. His sandy blond hair looked more disheveled than it had earlier, pieces sticking out of his ponytail. He stuck his hand forward for me to shake. It was cold. "Were you just outside?" I asked.

"Uh, for just a moment. I was getting something out of the garage," he said, running his hand through his hair. "How can I help you?"

"We need to speak to you about a matter that's been brought to our attention," I explained.

"Regarding?" Mathias raised his eyebrow.

"Regarding the recently deceased police chief." I crossed my arms.

Mathias looked around. "Why don't you come sit down in the dining room." Michaela and I followed him inside and took our seats across from him.

"What do you want to know?"

"Hunter! Michaela!" William clapped his hands as he walked into the room. "How wonderful to see you again so soon."

"Thank you, William," Michaela said, but I didn't pull my attention away from Mathias. Anne followed shortly behind her husband and sat next to Michaela.

"I understand you called the police chief several times before his death, berating him about his incompetence," I said.

"How did you hear about that?" asked Mathias.

William sat down next to his brother, across from Michaela. "Is that true?" he asked.

With his elbow on the table, Mathias rubbed his eyebrow. "I did."

"Why would you do that?" William asked, beating me to it. A knock sounded at the front door.

Mathias sat back and folded his arms. "I may have had too much to drink that night. Staring at all the family pictures, I blamed the police for not fixing this and finding Erik before it was too late."

"A manticore killed the police chief two days later," I reminded him.

"It wasn't me. I didn't kill him," he said, pointing to his chest. "I was at home."

"Sir," said the woman who had answered the door earlier, interrupting us. "Someone just dropped off this note. Said it was urgent." She handed it to William. The man's usual rosy-cheeked schoolboy face fell. With stricken eyes, he glanced at his brother before passing the note to me.

It wasn't very long, but the words hit me square in the chest.

"What does it say?" Michaela whispered beside me. The sound of her voice ripped my heart open. I would have crumpled the note and thrown it away if I thought it would stop her from reading it. So I didn't struggle when she plucked the paper from my hand. Her gasp didn't surprise me. I'd felt the same shock in my body when I had read the words:

Give us Michaela and no one else gets hurt.

Thirteen

Hunter

Michaela's smile dropped, and my anger rose. "Who gave you this note?" I barked at the woman standing next to William.

She did not flinch. "A boy rang the doorbell and handed me the note. Said it was urgent and said Michaela was to meet them at the Stave Church in one hour."

"Is the boy still here?" asked William. He had lost his usual merriment and concern creased his eyes.

"No. He ran off before I could question him further," she explained. "However, he looked like one of the boys employed at the butcher shop. The one owned by the Larsens."

Who knew that Michaela was here? And why would they want her?

If they thought of using my wife to extort me, I would not hand her over to them.

"They must be out of their minds, if they think I would let them have Michaela," I growled at no one in particular, but my eyes fell toward Mathias.

His face was blank and his hands steepled in front of his lips. "I don't think this is an empty threat," he said.

"This entire ordeal is just dreadful," said William, wringing his hands. "I don't understand why someone would want to do something like this." His wife placed her hands on top of his and he grasped them gently.

"If this is some kind of turf war, this may be a warning to your family that you are not untouchable," Michaela said to William. "Sending this note while we are here with your family could be a show of strength and defiance."

"That sounds conceivable to me," said Mathias, even though she had not addressed him directly.

"What can we do?" asked William.

Michaela's theory had merit. I quickly formed a plan in my mind. "William, you and Mathias come with me to the Stave Church and meet this predator. I will need backup since he may not be working alone."

"But he asked for me," Michaela whispered beside me.

I nodded. "You must come, too. But just like when our army attacked Elenora, I need you to wait until it is safe to come out." I saw the stubborn tilt of her jaw, but she did not respond.

"We will come with you," said William, and I noticed Mathias did not respond. "And you, Mathias?"

"I'm not exactly inclined to run into any trouble tonight."

"Mathias!" William scolded. But I raised my hand to stop him.

"You are not just taking part in some street brawl; this is for your kingdom and your people."

My words didn't seem to inspire Mathias's sense of honor. I wondered if he had any. I tried something else.

"If the Larsens are behind this, you would be the one to help me take them down," I said.

That seemed to prick his sense of duty. He nodded. "I may enjoy flexing who is the dominant family around here," he replied, then snuck a glance at Michaela.

"Good. We are all in agreement. Now, where do we find this church?"

Michaela

The Stave Church was not too far from the Pedersen's home but Hunter wasted no time leaving the mansion. He said he wanted to watch for anyone approaching before the appointed hour. As we drove up a hill, I soon realized this church was like none I'd ever seen before. It was five stories high and designed with at least ten peaks that I could see, several adorned with dragon heads and a bell tower situated inside the highest peak. The building was chestnut brown with several grey thatched roofs. William told me there were several Stave Churches throughout Norway and many, like this one, dated back to the twelfth century. They had been restored over the years and some still held religious services on the weekend, while others were repurposed into museums.

I expected the large wooden door to creak when Hunter pulled the handle, but it swung open without a sound. Inside, wooden columns and arches lined the perimeter, and the creak I had expected earlier finally sounded when I walked across the wooden floor. The church smelled of pine, of course, but it also had a lingering scent of paint. I thought it must have been from staining the wood to preserve it.

I spun around in a circle, taking in the building's beauty. I walked toward the altar positioned at the back, draped with a white cloth. But Hunter grabbed my hand before I could reach it. "Come with me," he said, and I followed him up a narrow staircase.

When I landed on the top step, I saw a mezzanine near the back where I imagined a choir singing above the congregation. Hunter tried to open the window at the top of the staircase, but it didn't budge and after a few minutes of gazing out into the open field surrounding the church, he walked to the opposite end to do the same thing on the other side.

"Do you see anything?" I asked. Hunter shook his head but continued to stare out the window. Other than me waiting upstairs, I didn't know how Hunter wanted to handle this. "What's your plan?"

Hunter looked over the mezzanine this time and onto the main floor. "There's only one entrance into the church and the windows on the upper floor don't seem to open. We essentially have him surrounded in here."

"What do you plan to do with him once he's inside?"

"I don't think he'll be much of a talker, but I will try to speak to him first."

I nodded, but then I placed my hand on Hunter's cheek and directed him to look at me. "If I feel, at any time, that he's not responding to your attempt at a conversation or he makes an obvious move for you, I will not hesitate to take him down."

He smiled. "I'm counting on it." Then he put both hands on either side of my face and leaned down to press his mouth against mine. I closed my eyes and breathed in his woodsy fragrance. Brushing my fingers through his hair, he dropped his hand to my lower back to push me closer. I moaned into his mouth and he gently bit my lower lip. I smiled and pulled a fistful of his hair. A growl rumbled in his chest, but his grin told me he loved it. He ran his tongue slowly across my lip just before...

"Someone's coming," Mathias whispered from below.

Headlights flooded the main floor of the church. Then the light was gone. The sun had nearly set, and the church was quite dark now. "Hunter, what if I don't see him make a move for you?" I panicked.

"Don't worry, Michaela, everything will be just fine."

I hated when people said things like that. I always thought it tempted fate to prove it would be exactly the opposite of fine.

"Hunter, he's coming," said William.

After a swift kiss on my lips, Hunter took the staircase two at a time and waited at the bottom of the steps for the assailant to arrive. I scanned the main floor and spotted William's light hair under the window next to the altar, then a movement caught my attention near the door. It was Mathias who stepped forward to open it.

It did not surprise the man on the other side to see him, as he simply walked through the entrance. His boots pounded against the wooden floor and he strode in like an outlaw from some western. He wore a short black leather jacket, and while I couldn't be sure, he reminded me of the manticore I had detected in the hotel bar lobby with Nicholas. *Has he been following me since I arrived in Norway?*

The manticore took a loud breath in through his nostrils and circled the room. "Where is she?" he asked.

Hunter stepped forward from behind the shadows to face him. "Did you really think I would let you take my wife?" he said.

"The thought crossed our minds. We aren't sure how attached you are to the human girl."

"We?" asked Hunter.

The man smiled. "I know she's here. I can smell her sweet perfume."

A heard a growl from below but I wasn't sure who made the sound. My guess was Hunter. "What do you want with her?" He took a step forward. "You have me here now. No need to play games any longer."

"Cocky bastard. This isn't about you."

What? This wasn't about Hunter; it was about me. But I didn't know the guy. I'd never been to Norway before. *How could this be about me?*

"What are you talking about?" asked Hunter, disbelief clear in his voice.

"We want the girl and if she will not come with us tonight, we'll just have to keep killing until she submits," he growled. He looked up toward the mezzanine and I quickly hid behind a column. Heavy footsteps pounded against the wooden floor. I chanced a peek at the scene below, but it was a mistake. Our eyes met, and the assailant smiled.

"There she is," he teased. Then he was gone in a flash. The snarls of two angry predators rang in my ears. Hunter's growl and the assailant's grunts echoed in the church. Confused, I crouched against the column, listening to the fight below.

Footsteps stomped up the staircase. A shout, Hunter's, rang out before two bodies slammed down at the top of the stairs. Hunter held the assailant by the leg, but he spun onto his back and kicked Hunter off of him. I worried whether I should help yet.

"Hunter, what do you want me to do?" I pleaded.

"Stay out of it!" he said. "Get back." I ran to the end of the mezzanine where the choir would have sat and watched as Hunter struggled to get his hands around the assailant's throat. He turned his head to gnash at Hunter's wrists but came up short. His fangs were long and thick. I could see them from the back of the room. Then the assailant jerked his knee up, knocking the wind out of Hunter.

It was enough for Hunter to loosen his grip on the man's throat and he escaped. Catching sight of me, he didn't hesitate. He raced down the mezzanine faster than any other manticore I'd ever seen. He was in front of me in the time it took for me to blink twice. I stood there like a fly caught in a spider's web, nowhere to run and nowhere to hide. I didn't have enough time to say or think anything before he grabbed my waist and hoisted me up over his shoulder. Closing my eyes, I listened to his heartbeat. It was as loud as a drum against my ear: ba-ba-boom. This time, I did not hesitate.

I imagined squeezing his heart, cutting the blood off from the valve. His heartbeat faltered. I could barely hear it now at all. The assailant stumbled back but still gripped me to his shoulder. I readied the words that would stop his heart completely and whispered them. *Vita dans cor. Desine iam. Life giving heart. Stop now.*

The words tumbled from my lips. His heart would stop any second now. I felt the warrior in me celebrate. Opening my eyes, I turned to see Hunter racing toward us. I wanted to signal to him that I would be okay. I had this. But instead of triumph, I saw horror painted across Hunter's face. Still over the assailant's shoulder, I swiveled my head to look behind me and saw the banister only a second before the assailant and I fell two stories down.

"No!" screamed Hunter at the same time that I shouted his name and reached forward to grab his hand. He caught my ring finger, and the temporary relief I had felt fizzled with the stunning realization that I was still going to fall. His sweaty fingers slipped the ring off, and I fell backward, my arms and legs flailing with nothing left to grab onto.

I screamed, but it sounded far away even to my own ears.

"Michaela!" shouted Hunter.

As I fell, the sight of Hunter on his knees at the edge of the broken banister burned my eyes. His arms outstretched, shouting at the top of his lungs. His red face, marred by throbbing veins, was the last thing I saw before I closed my eyes and prepared myself for the impact below.

"Oof!" I huffed when I hit a hard body. Then a loud crash resounded beside me.

"I got you," said William, legs teetering as he steadied himself from the jolt of my body crashing into his waiting arms.

"Oh my God, William," I heaved, panting and out of breath. "I thought I was going to die." I looked for Hunter. He wasn't at the mezzanine any longer, but footsteps hammered down the stairs. He raced toward me and stole me from William's arms to hold me in his. With a hand to the back of my head, he held my face against his chest, his heartbeat pulsating across my cheek. I thought it would pop out of his sternum.

"Get that body out of here," he growled and wouldn't let me go from his arms even when I tried to catch a glimpse of the man.

"Don't," he whispered when I attempted to turn my face. "You don't want to see this," he said.

I believed him. It was enough to know the man was dead; I didn't need to see his broken body in my nightmares.

The sound of boots thumping along the wooden floor was all the sign I had that someone was moving the body. A door opening then a loud thump as someone pushed the body down the front stairs. Hunter finally let me go. He pulled me away from his chest but held my face between the palm of his hands.

"Are you okay?" he asked.

I nodded. Still shaking from fear and relief, I managed to speak. "I'm okay," I assured him.

"Does anything hurt? Did you hit something when you fell? Did he bite you?" He started pulling up my sleeves and tearing down my shirt from my neck.

I shook my head. "No," he didn't touch me, other than to grab me."

"I don't think he was trying to kill her," said Mathias, returning from outside. "He would have just done it when he grabbed her. Instead, he wanted to carry her out of here. Safe to say, they want you—but they want you alive. At least until you get to where they have to take you. They'll probably kill you after that."

A growl rumbled in Hunter's chest, and his snarl revealed his fangs. He closed his eyes.

"Shut up, Mathias," William whispered harshly. The first time I'd seen his face angry. Mathias simply shrugged, keeping a cautious eye on Hunter, nonetheless.

"He's right," Hunter said, opening his eyes. His breathing even once again. "Which means this isn't over, even with a body count. This one was just a goon, someone sent to take Michaela to the real culprit. This isn't some insane manticore. I think we're dealing with someone more strategic than that."

"What do we do now?" I asked.

"We follow our lead."

"Which is?" I prodded.

"Alexander Larsen," he responded. "Vivienne could have accidentally told Alexander where we were going tonight."

I nodded. "You're right."

Hunter climbed into the car, but I stood on the church steps. "Are you coming?"

I jogged down the steps and got inside the car. I was about to ask where they put the assailant's body but decided it was better that I didn't know.

Fourteen

Michaela

Hunter drove us out of the church parking lot and onto the gravel path road. "I should go to the hotel room to change before we meet with Alexander," I said to Hunter, fastening my seatbelt on the passenger side. William and Mathias sat in the back.

"You almost died tonight, Michaela. I think you should stay back at the hotel and rest." Hunter kept his eyes on the road.

"What?" I asked, surprised that he would try to leave me behind again. "I thought we were in this together. No more secrets."

"We are, but we don't need four people to question Alexander. I promise to fill you in on the entire conversation when I get back."

"You need William and Mathias, but not me?" I asked, knowing it sounded peevish, but my nerves were shot. I turned back to the manticores behind me. "No offense."

William put his hands up, but Mathias stared out his window.

"Yes. Bringing William and Mathias will show dominance and I need all the advantages I can get right now. I want to take care of this tonight."

I blew out a breath. I felt exhausted, barely able to lift my limbs. Why was I arguing about going to speak to some power-hungry manticore rather than falling asleep in a warm bed? "Fine," I sighed. "But tell me everything when you get back. No more trying to protect me."

"Agreed. But one more thing," he said.

"Why do I get the feeling I won't like it?" I turned in my seat to watch his facial expression.

He cast me a sideways glance and said, "Call Nicholas and ask him to stay with you."

I sighed loudly this time. "I don't need a babysitter, Hunter. I'm a grown woman."

"I know you are, trust me," he said, and his gaze raked over my body. That improved my temperament. "I don't think anyone will try to kidnap you at the hotel. There are too many security cameras. However, someone may try to get in through the window. I want someone watching over you while you rest. Please, Michaela. I can't concentrate if I'm worried about your safety."

It sounded like a reasonable plan, so I nodded. I pulled out my phone and found Nicholas's number. "Hey, Nicholas," I said when he answered. "Where are you?" I checked my watch and it was nearly ten. Is Vivienne still with you?"

"Oh hi, Michaela. I'm at the hotel. Vivienne just dropped me off."

"Would you mind staying with me tonight?" I asked.

"Of course. Is everything all right? Where's Hunter?"

I looked up and stared at my husband. His dark hair caught the street lamp's reflection and cast a dark shadow over his features. Perhaps it wasn't the effects of the light, and he was just worried. "Hunter's fine. I'm fine. I'll catch you up when I see you. I should be there in twenty minutes."

"See you soon," he said, and I ended the call. Hunter reached over the console and grabbed my hand. Resigned to the fact that I was heading back to the hotel to rest, all the adrenaline from tonight seeped through my veins and drained me. I sat back and closed my eyes for just a minute.

***

"Michaela, we're here." Hunter's voice drifted in my ear. I remembered another time he'd said the same thing to me. The scent of the salty ocean tickled my nose, and I wiggled my toes, imagining the sand in between them. "Michaela." Someone shook me. The sky was soft indigo and I quickly realized I wasn't in Italy but Norway.

"Wow, we got to the hotel quickly," I said, straightening out of my seat.

"You slept the entire time," said Hunter. His familiar grin warmed the cool air inside the car.

"I guess I did," I yawned and turned to face the backseat. "Thank you for saving me, William."

"Don't mention it," he said, a blush rising on his fair skin. Mathias grumbled something underneath his breath. "Goodnight, Mathias," was all I could muster to him. I turned back to Hunter and placed both my hands on his cheeks and kissed him. "Be safe."

"You too," he replied. When I moved to step out of the car, he pulled me back and kissed me harder this time. His fingers at the back of my head curled and the tip of his blunt nails on my scalp gave me shivers. "Wait up for me," he whispered. I smiled and sashayed out of the car. Yup, I swayed my hips back and forth because I knew it would torture him. I heard the growl right before the squeal of the tires. Hunter sped off, and I grinned knowing he'd be thinking of me even though I wasn't with him.

I greeted the door attendant and nearly walked right into Nicholas. "Nicholas, I wasn't expecting you in the lobby but I'm glad you're here."

Nicholas pulled me into his embrace and patted my back. "You look terrible. What happened?"

I snorted softly, but then looked down at my clothes. I still had pieces of sawdust from the broken banister all over my black sweater. I tried to dust it off, but the pieces stuck to the fabric. Despite everything I'd been through tonight, I didn't want to sleep anymore and I didn't want to cram myself inside a hotel room. "Will you have a drink with me at the bar?"

Nicholas looked at the bar, then at me. "Are you sure? It's pretty crowded in there."

"Yes. I want to be surrounded by people. Feel alive and enjoy the good things in life, like a nice glass of wine."

He chuckled and stuck out his elbow. I wrapped my arm around his as he escorted me to the bar. "What can I get you?" he asked when we took our seats on the black leather stools. I placed my elbows on the mirrored counter and took stock of the bar. "Mmm, maybe just a white wine."

"Two Pinot Grigio," said Nicholas to the bartender, holding up two fingers. It wasn't very loud in the bar, only a soft hum of conversation and a piano melody playing in the background, so his signal wasn't necessary. I smiled at his consideration, though. "Thank you again for coming to Norway and sticking around. You really have been like a second father to me." Whether it was the emotions of the night catching up to me or the memory of my late father running through my mind, a tear fell down my cheek and I quickly wiped it away.

"Hey, don't cry," crooned Nicholas. He placed his hand on top of mine at the bar. "Coming here means as much to me as it does to you."

I lifted my head to look at him. "It does?"

He smiled. "You're not like your mother," he said, and I felt guilty at the satisfaction and joy those words gave me. My mother was a manticore slayer and made some mistakes in her life. While I understood why she did it, I didn't like being compared to her. So hearing Nicholas, one of the closest people to my mother, say that I wasn't like her, well... It was a relief.

"Your mother never trusted me enough to bring me with her on missions," he said, looking down at our hands clasped at the bar.

"I don't think it was you she didn't trust," I said. "My mother had a tough time trusting anyone," I explained. "Since she was a child, my grandmother warned her that there would be people looking for her and wanting to exploit her. She had learned to depend on herself and not share the burden with others. I wouldn't take it personally, Nicholas."

"Perhaps," he said. "I'd never thought about it that way." He patted my hand and brought his hand up to rest against his cheek, his elbow firmly on the bar. "I remember the way she would look at my father, though," added Nicholas. "It was as if the sun and the moon rose with every word he said."

"Yes, Signora Tassone mentioned something like that," I recalled. Signora Tassone lived next door to my mother when she would visit Nicholas's father in Italy. "He was the first one who told her the truth about what she was truly capable of. I could see how she would develop a hero-worship of him."

The bartender discreetly passed a few napkins our way. I appreciated the gesture as I'd run out of tissues.

"I guess I'd assumed after my father passed away that I would take over his role in guiding her on her missions," he said. "But it didn't quite work out that way. She accepted the intel I would give her, but I rarely knew what her next move would be. Sometimes I wonder if I did, maybe I could have saved her. Perhaps if I knew how to get a hold of the manticore king, I could have saved your mother's life that day."

"There's no point in beating ourselves up with what-ifs. We can't control how others perceive us. We can only control our own actions. You did the best you could for my mother and I love you for that, Nicholas."

Nicholas sniffed and hid it behind a cough, bringing his hand up to cover his face. "Yes, well, it's good to feel useful and I'm proud to have you call me whenever you need me. Adam opened his own dojo, and Olivia started a new job with the local police. The hotel business in Italy keeps me busy but being needed keeps me alive."

I nodded, understanding the sentiment. Knowing Hunter and Violet needed me kept me going even when things got tough.

Wanting to get away from this melancholy mood, I clapped my hands and turned my chair toward him. "So, tell me where you went with Vivienne."

"Oh, what an extraordinary young lady," said Nicholas.

I frowned. "Well, you realize she's not really ordinary."

"True," he chuckled. "She took me to a place near the east coast of Norway. We watched the midnight sun from there. It was incredible. The sun never set, its rays constricting down to a sliver, only to expand again a few minutes later. It was magical."

"Yes, this whole place has a very spellbinding sentiment around it. I can feel it too."

Nicholas's stare grew somber. "What happened tonight that you asked me here with you?"

At that moment, the bartender delivered our glasses of wine. I was glad because I was going to need the fortitude.

"I almost died," I said and took a sip of my wine.

Nicholas shook his head. "You sure know how to start a story," he said, and I laughed. Then I told him about the Pedersens, the note and the manticore Hunter was confronting tonight. Nicholas sat back and listened to me patiently. He held my hand and rubbed my back, just like I had always imagined my father would do.

Fifteen

Michaela

No matter where I was or how tired I felt, I maintained my nightly face washing ritual. Ever since I was a teenager at sleepovers or late college nights, I always washed my face before crashing face-first onto my pillow.

Despite my exhaustion, I padded barefoot across the hotel room floor and stood in front of the bathroom mirror. Rummaging through my overnight bag, I pulled out my bottles. With a cotton pad, I wiped off my makeup, then pumped a dime-size amount of cleanser onto my fingers, rubbing the transparent liquid between my hands before covering my face with the sudsy soap.

I had just washed the cleanser off and was applying my night cream when my cell phone rang. I checked the digital alarm clock on the nightstand on my way to grab my phone lying on the bed. It was nearly two in the morning.

Hunter's name scrolled across my screen. I swiped right with my finger to answer the call. "Hello?"

"Michaela, are you all right?"

"Yes, I'm fine," I said, rubbing the moisturizer off of my fingers while balancing the phone on my shoulder. "Are you on your way back? How did it go with Alexander?"

"Fine, fine," he said, sounding rushed. "Is Nicholas there with you?"

"Don't get mad, but I sent him home. The windows don't open

and we're on the 18th floor. I promised I wouldn't open the door to anyone. He looked so tired and I couldn't ask him to stay here all night while I slept. He left about half an hour ago." I rubbed the side of my face near my ear as I'd felt a bit of cream still on there.

Hunter swore violently into the phone, and my heart stopped. I stood up from the bed slowly. "What's going on?" When he didn't respond, I knew it was bad. "Dammit, Hunter, tell me what's happened!" I shouted.

I heard Hunter inhale a deep breath before he continued. "After speaking with Alexander, I went back to the Pedersen mansion to drop off Mathias and William."

"Okay..."

"Shortly after we returned, another note arrived."

My heart raced now. "What did the note say?"

Hunter blew out the breath he'd been holding. "It said: Come to the church alone this time or Nicholas dies."

"What?" I whispered, air whooshing out of my lungs, forcing me to sit back down onto the bed. With my hand on my chest, fighting the pain in my lungs, I said, "But he just left here, not that long ago."

"They must have been waiting outside of the hotel for him."

"This is all my fault," I began.

"This isn't your fault."

A thought popped up in my mind. "Alexander knew you had to go back to the Pedersen's house to drop off William and Mathis, right? Maybe he didn't want to risk sending the note to the hotel and sent it there instead. He was the only one who knew you were going back there."

"Maybe," said Hunter in a low voice.

I paced the hotel room, running my hands through my hair. I knew Hunter would not like my next words, but it needed to happen. "I have to go back to the church. Alone, this time," I told him.

"No way," he said, as I expected.

"Hunter, if the same person who committed those brutal murders has Nicholas, I can't risk anything like that happening to him. I have to go alone."

"I can't let you do that," he growled. "There is nothing in this world—manticore, beast or god—that can keep me from that church."

"I'm telling you this, not as a god but as your wife," I whispered.

"Don't do this," he said, and his voice sounded unsteady. "Don't make me wait here not knowing what will happen to you."

"We don't have a choice," I cried, tears falling down my cheeks. "They'll kill him. I can't lose him. I've already lost too much." I wiped the tears from my face. "I have to do this alone." I inhaled a deep breath and said, "Goodbye, Hunter."

"Michaela, wait!" he shouted, but I ended the call. I knew it was a terrible gesture, but nothing he could say would change my mind. I couldn't save my parents, but I'd be damned if I didn't try everything in my power to save Nicholas.

I grabbed my jacket and laced up my boots. I didn't have a weapon. I didn't need one. I would take care of this manticore problem the only way I knew how—with my chants.

I'd called a taxi and spotted the car waiting outside of the hotel when I reached the lobby. Hunter mentioned someone may have grabbed Nicholas outside of the hotel. Looking around, I didn't see anyone suspicious. I knew it would look ridiculous, but I didn't want to take any chances. I darted through the lobby, burst through the front doors, and jumped into the taxi. "Go, go!" I shouted to the driver. He looked frazzled, but he put the car into drive and sped away.

"Where are we going, ma'am?" he asked when he reached the road.

I turned around and peered through the back window, watching the hotel get further away in the distance. No one was chasing after us and no speeding car trailed behind us. I blew out a breath and turned back into my seat. "Please take me to the Stave Church, the one by the coast."

The driver nodded, and I concentrated on slowing down my racing heart. I needed to remain calm and focused right now. Closing my eyes, I planned out what I would do when I reached the church. I knew I could handle this. Back in New York, I'd fought an army of manticores before with a single chant. I could handle whatever I faced tonight. They had no idea whom they were dealing with. The pep talk was working. I was ready by the time the taxi pulled up in front of the church. I looked around and saw no other cars around.

"Are you sure this is where you want me to drop you off?" asked the driver, looking around the empty parking lot. "I don't think the church is even open."

"It's open," I said, recalling we'd left it that way only hours ago. I paid him and climbed out of the backseat.

"Good luck, ma'am," he said. I smiled at his concern before he drove away. When I could no longer see the car, I ran up the church steps and pulled open the heavy wooden door. Still no creak. Walking slowly inside, heel to toe against the oak floors, I stopped when I reached the main room. Broken pieces of banister lay on the floor. No one had come back to clean it up. I moved closer to the wreckage and picked up the pieces of wood, moving them off to the side. Lifting my head, I saw the opening that wasn't supposed to be there but that our bodies had created when we crashed through the railing. I shivered at the memory. I couldn't believe I was back here so soon. Thankfully, my legs felt strong, and I told myself I could handle this. I could handle anything.

Just then, light filled the room, and I knew a car approached. I raced to the second floor to watch whoever wanted me dead step out of the car. When I saw the manticore climb out, anger boiled inside of me. "No," I said. The word rose deep from the pit of my stomach. My fists curled by my sides. "I told him to stay back." I was so angry at Hunter; I almost didn't see the second car approach. *He even brought reinforcements.*

"Michaela!" Hunter shouted when he stormed through the front doors.

I inhaled deeply through my nostrils and exhaled roughly through my mouth. I did this three times before I heard him race up the stairs.

"Michaela, where are you?"

"I'm. Right. Here," I ground out, enunciating each word. Releasing my fists, I prepared to pepper him with every angry word I had in my vocabulary. "I told you not to come."

His dark head popped over the staircase and he turned to find me next to the window. He reached me in two strides and pulled me into his arms. I stiffened and didn't move my arms to return the embrace.

"I know you're mad at me," he said, stroking my hair as he held me tightly against his body.

"Oh, I'm more than mad at you, Hunter," I said.

"I know." He pulled away and put his hands on my cheeks. "But I'd rather spend every day for the rest of my life apologizing to you than regretting my decision."

"Hunter—"

"Someone else is here," William interrupted with a shout from the front of the church.

"I thought the other car coming up the road was with you," I said.

Hunter shook his head. "No. I came with the Pedersen brothers. I don't know who the other car is."

"Well, we're about to find out," I said. "William, Mathias, hide yourselves. I don't want him to know that anyone else is here."

"Michaela, he will know other manticores are here, he can sense them, we all can," Hunter reminded me.

"What if it's not a manticore?"

Hunter pursed his lips, not seeming to think that possible.

We were out of time to discuss this. I placed my hands on Hunter's arms and squeezed. "I'm heading down there to talk to him. If there's no reasoning with him, I will let him take me to Nicholas. I have to find out where they're holding him."

Hunter grabbed my arm as I tried to go downstairs. "No," he growled. "They will not let you see him. It's only a trap to get to you. This may be personal with the kingdom."

"I don't care what this is about anymore. Right now, I only care about getting Nicholas out."

While Hunter and I argued upstairs, the front doors of the church burst open. Footsteps stomped across the foyer and a voice boomed, "I know you're not alone, Michaela. I can smell your pets."

Hunter raised his eyebrow at me, and I shook my head at him.

"What do you want?" I shouted.

"Why, you, of course, I thought we made that quite clear." The man was in the middle of the church now and his red hair caught the light. He wore a green coat and brown pants. I couldn't see his eyes from up here, but if he could smell the other manticores in the room, he was one of them. When he reached the front of the church, he stopped to look down at the wreckage. "I guess now we know what happened to the other guy."

He must have felt my eyes on the back of his neck because his head shot up, and he looked in my direction. I hid behind a column again but heard him swear softly under his breath.

"If you will not follow the rules and come out and play, Michaela, then I have no choice. I must head back to deal with Nicholas." He strode toward the foyer, approaching the front doors.

"Mathias, stop him!" Hunter shouted when the man reached for the handle.

Mathias stood in front of the door, blocking the exit, but the manticore picked him up, just like a ragdoll, and threw him across the room. His head hit the wooden wall, and he slumped down unconscious.

"Mathias!" William yelled and jumped onto the other manticore's shoulders.

The red-haired manticore roared and arched his back, shaking William off of him as though he weighed nothing at all.

William didn't give up. He punched the other manticore, but either his puffy coat softened the blow or this beast was indestructible. He turned around and, with one swift punch in the gut, William fell to his knees, panting for air. The redhead turned and walked out.

A loud growl shook the wooden rafters and Hunter raced down the church aisle, then out the front door after him.

"Wait!" I hollered and held the wall as I ran down the staircase. William was already back up and pulled the door open for me to go first.

Hunter had the man pinned against a car. But then the other manticore pulled out a syringe and stabbed Hunter in the neck with it.

"No!" I screamed.

The man's gaze connected with mine and I saw the moment he hesitated, wondering if he could take me too. I closed my eyes to begin a chant, but before I could think of stopping his heart, the manticore threw Hunter and himself into the backseat and slammed the car door shut. The driver revved the engine and the tires squealed as the car sped off into the night.

I stood there, horrified and confused.

"They wanted me!" I shouted. "Why didn't they take me?"

My legs shook and I dropped to my knees in the middle of the parking lot, staring at the violet sky on the horizon. William put his arm around me. He tried to comfort me, but I couldn't feel anything. The plan hadn't worked. They took Hunter, and it was all because of me. I'd thought I could handle anything, but I wasn't prepared for that.

Sixteen

Michaela

I was still kneeling on the ground, staring out into the starless night sky, when William pulled himself up and stood next to me.

"Will you be all right for a moment, Michaela?" he asked. "I need to go inside and check on my brother."

I nodded once but gave no other response. With a squeeze on my shoulder, William rose and his footsteps sounded on the pavement behind me until silence blanketed me.

Think Michaela! Where could they have taken him?

No matter how hard I tried, I couldn't think of a single place.

Vivienne.

Vivienne spoke to Alexander Larsen; she would know how to get a hold of him. She didn't believe Alexander had anything to do with this, but I needed to find out for sure. I picked myself off the ground and walked back to the church.

As soon as I stepped inside, I spotted William helping his brother to his feet. Mathias struggled to get up, but his eyes connected with mine and they narrowed. He probably wasn't happy to have been knocked out, protecting a human. I would not apologize. Besides, I had a bigger problem. I didn't have Vivienne's phone number.

"William, I need you to call Vivienne for me," I told him. "You do know who she is?" Vivienne had said she knew all the influential families in Norway.

"She works at the academy, correct?"

"Yes."

William kept his arm around Mathias's back until he was sure his brother could stand on his own. "Anne has her number. We will call her as soon as we return to the house."

Desperate to be on my way to search for Hunter, I walked over to help William get Mathias inside the car. But Mathias held up his hand when I approached. "I'm fine. I can walk to the car on my own."

Relieved rather than offended, I opened the church door and watched him walk right past me. He got into the back seat of William's car and left the front seat open for me. I guess I should have been happy but feeling Mathias's stare at the back of my neck made me more uncomfortable. I would have preferred to ride in the backseat.

Fortunately, it wasn't a long drive back to the house and William had already called Anne, asking her to search for Vivienne's number. I wasted no time when I reached the house and asked Anne to dial the number. She had it readied on her phone.

"Hello?" Vivienne answered after two rings.

"Vivienne. This is Michaela. Hunter is gone. I need to speak to Alexander. I need—"

"Wait! What happened to Hunter?" she asked.

"They took him," my voice cracked, and I tried to steady my nerves. "And I have no idea where to find him." A sob escaped, and I covered my mouth. "Please. I need to speak to Alexander right now."

"All right. Meet me at *Lexi's*," said Vivienne. "I'll be there in twenty minutes." Then she ended the call. I turned to Anne. "Will you take me?"

She nodded and turned to her husband. "Will you join us?"

"I will get Mathias settled into his room and meet you both there if I can," he said and kissed her brow. Anne caught up to me in the hallway and grabbed her coat as we headed out.

I'd only been around manticores for about a year, but I had met hundreds in that short time. I'd never, however, met a manticore as timid as Anne. I wondered if her life experiences had shaped her this way or if it was simply her personality. I'd always raced toward what I wanted and thought about the consequences later. "Thank you for taking me, Anne," I said when I sat in the passenger seat of her car.

"Of course," she replied, but her voice was uneven and her hands shook while she adjusted the rearview mirror. She pulled the seatbelt across her lap and gripped the steering wheel. Then nodded and started the engine.

Hunter

Pain shot through every muscle in my body. They had strapped my legs and arms to some medieval contraption, pulling my muscles from limb to limb. I wanted to shout out, but I held it in, reserving every ounce of my strength. When I denied them the reaction they craved, they came for blood. The biggest one, T*he Mammoth*, they had called him, walked up to me now. He pulled his fist back and slammed it straight into my ribs.

Fuuuck, I shouted in my head. But I bit my lip, refraining myself from screaming it aloud. Instead, I panted and inhaled deep breaths, preparing for the next assault. He didn't disappoint. He hit me again, on the left side of my rib cage this time, then again, harder still, connecting with my kidneys.

"Coward," I panted. "Twice my size and you still have to fight me while I'm tied up."

The Mammoth growled and raised both of his fists. I was certain, this time, he would actually break through the rib cage with his force. I braced myself for the impact and hoped I would heal from the injury.

"Stop!" shouted a voice who had just entered the room. "He is no use to us dead."

The Mammoth brought his arms down and sneered at me. "I'll come back to finish this later."

A man wearing a light grey suit came into view. He stared down at me, and I stared back into his amber eyes. I recognized him instantly.

"It was you," I spit out.

"Yes," he sighed, putting his hands in his pockets. "So now you finally know."

"You had sat only a few inches away from me. I should have killed you when I had the chance."

Seventeen

Hunter

Anger raged inside of me, lengthening my incisors. “Hans Pedersen, *you bastard.*”

He nodded and walked along the perimeter of the darkened room. Catching my breath, I turned my head, taking in my surroundings. The walls were made of stone and the ground was plain dirt. Only a couple of gas lamps were lit, not enough for this enormous space. He had brought me to some cave to torture me. “Why are you doing this?”

“I want your wife.”

His words hurt me more than *The Mammoth* had.

“Why risk everything, the wrath of my father and mine, for a human?” I asked.

He smirked, then paced the room with his hands interlaced behind his back.

I gritted my teeth.

“For two decades, I couldn’t understand it. How had a human woman done it?”

“Done what?” I asked, confused.

He sighed, his impatience seeping through his taunt jaw. “Let me start at the beginning. Are you paying attention, Hunter?”

I grunted.

“Erik was a rebellious child. Never wanted to toe the line. If he wanted something, he would simply take it.” Hans grabbed a wooden chair in the corner of the dark cave and sat down, back straight.

"My wife tried her best to raise him right, but he grew meaner as the years went on. It frustrated him that he couldn't use his superior physical strength in competitions. It would bring attention to himself and those were the rules handed down by your father–by all means necessary we had to keep our existence a secret. Erik hated being told what to do and what not to do." He looked up at the ceiling.

"When I realized I wasn't getting through to him, I asked Astrid to speak to him. She did an adequate job keeping his instincts under control for a while, but then one night, some ignorant drunk human picked a fight with my son in a bar. Erik took it outside. He knocked the man out with a single punch. Unfortunately, he didn't stop there. He kept hitting him until he broke the man's face and limbs. Someone ran to get Astrid, but it was too late to save the man. Astrid said that Erik must face the consequences. He would have to turn himself in to the police."

"'I'll never be put behind bars,' he'd said. I reminded him he'd lived a long life, that a few years weren't so bad, and it'd be good practice to manage his unruly behavior. I thought we'd gotten through to him. He agreed to turn himself in to police the next morning. He just wanted one more night of freedom before being incarcerated. I convinced Astrid to give him one more night, and she reluctantly agreed." He stood.

"Erik did not turn himself in the next morning. In fact, he never returned. He had fled the country, and we didn't know where he'd gone. Soon after, rumors started, and then news reports of horrific homicides across Europe. Astrid was sure it was Erik, but I couldn't be convinced. She alerted the king, who sent men to track down Erik and bring him home. But Erik never came home."

"Did my father kill him? If so, what does this have to do with Michaela?"

"No, your father's men never reached Erik. A human woman found him first and killed him. When Astrid told me, I was livid. How could this have happened? How could a human have killed my son?"

My heart stopped, but my brain plugged in the details. It came to the same conclusion my heart had already figured out. Lucia—Michaela's mom—killed his son. I closed my eyes and couldn't believe this was happening.

"I never knew who that woman was and why she'd killed Erik."

"How did you find out? Why now?"

"One of your family members visited me recently."

I racked my brain but couldn't think of a single member of my family that visited Norway recently. Laura produced indie movies and traveled a lot, but she hadn't come here. My uncle Davis traveled abroad last year. But it couldn't be him. He knew nothing of Michaela while he was traveling.

"Who was it?"

"*Elenora*," Hans whispered close to my ear.

I curled my hands into fists by my side. I shook my head and finally roared out in pain, "No!"

Stripped of her claws, her venom, and her instincts, Elenora had still found a way to hurt Michaela.

"Yes. She told me quite a bit about your bride and what she did to her." He walked away, but his voice still echoed in the dark room. "It all made sense. How a human could possibly take down a manticore. Because she wasn't entirely human, was she? She was a descendant of Egyptian gods."

I needed to think, to say something that would persuade him otherwise. "Elenora is a liar. She said those things because my father kicked her out of the kingdom for usurping his throne. She betrayed him and is a traitor to all manticores. You cannot trust her," I shouted and glared at him, willing him to believe me.

"You're right. Perhaps I cannot take her word," said Hans. "But I do trust my own eyes. And Elenora's blue ones do not lie. Nor do her short fingernails. Despite being attacked by another manticore, she could not fight back. I believe what she says to be true."

"What do you want?" I shouted, desperate to negotiate despite my anger. "It wasn't Michaela who killed Erik. I'm tired of these vengeful fathers placing blame at Michaela's feet when it's their anger-ridden sons who cannot control themselves."

"I do not seek revenge," he whispered. "I seek resurrection."

Resurrection?

"Over a month ago, the goddess Hel visited me in my dream," he explained. "She confirmed Erik was with her in Helheim and not Valhalla."

I shook my head, a little surprised that Hans still believed in the old gods. Ancient Norse mythology claimed only warriors that died in battle went to Valhalla, the others went to Helheim ruled by the goddess Hel. Once a soul passes into Helheim, it cannot return unless a deal is struck with the goddess.

"What did she ask of you?" I closed my eyes, anticipating the response.

"That I bring the blood of the woman who killed Erik to this altar." He ran his hands along the black stone block beside me. "A soul for a soul. Lucia's blood runs through Michaela's veins. I will have my son back," he said, his face inches away from mine.

"This won't bring back your son. It was just a dream." I argued. I recalled the legends saying Hel was the goddess of death. If she appeared in Han's dreams, it was a sign that his own death was imminent.

I hoped that was true.

But first, I had to convince him to leave Michaela alone. "You are not an evil man, Hans. This dream played havoc with your emotions. You went off the rails, but you are not a bad person. Think of all the good you and your wife have done with your charities."

"We did a lot. But it wasn't enough to bring back my son, was it?" He walked away, yet I heard him whisper, "And even good men do bad things, Hunter."

I couldn't help but recall my arms wrapped around Jenkins's neck right before I snapped it. I regretted nothing.

"I would argue then that we are not good," I said.

He smiled. "Does that bother you?"

My eye twitched because it didn't bother me. Not if it meant protecting the people I loved. I hated that we felt the same way.

"I won't let you do this," I told him. "If you touch one hair on her head—"

"Do your worst, Hunter." He said, moving away from me. "Because I will do mine."

I pulled at my constraints; the ropes tearing at my flesh. When they didn't break, I dropped my arms in defeat.

Closing my eyes, I imagined the things he could do to Michaela, and my eyes burned. I wished he had broken my ribs instead.

Eighteen

Michaela

Since Pedersen's home was closer to the coast than the city, it took us more than twenty minutes to reach Alexander's club. Just like the other night, the line to get in wrapped around the block. I walked right up to the entrance and didn't stop walking until a large hand wrapped itself around my arm.

"Hey! Where do you think you're going?" the hulk of a man near the entrance said as he pulled me back from the door.

"She's with me," said a timid voice behind me, and I turned to see Anne standing straight and prim, holding the strap of her purse at her shoulder. I didn't think the security guard noticed how white her knuckles were, but I did. "We're here to see Alexander Larsen," I explained, trying not to punch the guy in the mouth for slowing me down.

He looked Anne up and down for only a moment before he recognized her. I was sure the richest woman in the country trying to cut in line at your club didn't happen to him every day. "Um, is he expecting you, Ms. Pedersen?" His voice rose two octaves higher than when he shouted at me.

"Yes," Anne said. It was all the explanation she gave him. I took note that less was more in situations of authority.

"Kindly let go of my guest. Now," she told him. Although the guard was not a manticore, working for Alexander, he was probably used to being around them. However, there was something about Anne's assertiveness right now that made me smile.

"Yes, ma'am," he said and let go of me immediately.

"Where can we find Alexander?" Anne asked, tilting her head as she peered into the club.

"Take the stairs to your left to the second floor. You'll see another guard there; he'll take you to him."

"Thank you," she said crisply and sauntered into the club. I followed beside her. As soon as she turned the corner, she blew out a loud breath and her shoulders slumped forward. "Well, that went better than I had expected."

I laughed, and she smiled back at me. "You were incredible," I said and meant it. "Let's go find Alexander."

Another security guard met us as soon as we stepped onto the second floor. The one at the door must have warned him about us. His amber eyes seemed to peer through me, but as soon as the chill ran up my spine, he turned and led us down a dark hallway. Strobe lights pulsated against the walls and I spotted a balcony at the end of the corridor. We didn't make it that far because the guard stopped and knocked on the third door.

"Enter," said a gruff voice from inside.

The guard turned the knob and motioned us to go in first. I stepped forward and Anne was just behind me. As soon as she crossed the threshold, the door slammed shut. Anne jumped at the sound. I turned for only a second to confirm the guard was not standing behind us, then immediately turned back around to face Alexander. He wasn't alone. Vivienne sat beside him on a red leather couch. There was no one else in the room.

"Hello, Michaela," said Vivienne. "Good to see you, Anne."

I waited for Alexander to speak, but he said nothing. Although the room was dark, it was not difficult to notice his striking features. He had short, blond hair that looked clean and lightly tousled. His amber eyes pierced through the darkness and pulled me closer to him. Unintentionally, I stepped forward but halted when a smile curled upon his face. He moved his arresting stare behind me.

"Welcome, Anne," he drawled. "I must say, I am surprised to see you here." Anne didn't respond.

He smiled again, and I felt like a sheep caught by a wolf's gaze. "I take it you are the lovely Michaela Durand." His soft voice zinged through my body. "Rumors about you crossed the pond and have reached me all the way up here."

"I'm sure the news came to you a lot more direct than that," I said, staring pointedly at Vivienne.

He shook his head and turned to Vivienne. "It seems this human has larger claws than you do, my dear," he laughed.

Vivienne smiled but it looked more like a grimace.

I didn't want to play games with either of them. I wanted to get Hunter back now. "As I'm sure you've heard, Hunter was taken, and I need to find him." I paused when another thought wormed its way into my head. "I need to find him... alive."

Alexander smiled. "Smart woman to specify."

"They took Nicholas, too." I bit my lip to hold back my emotions. A small gasp escaped from Vivienne's lips.

I waited for Alexander to make the next move. He leaned forward on the couch and steepled his fingers together in front of his lips. "As I'm sure you know, the kingdom is offering a reward to anyone that can lead to the capture of the killer manticore."

I nodded again, unsure where he was going with this. He stared at me and smiled.

"What is the reward for returning the heir to the kingdom?" he asked.

Surprised by his question, I scrambled. "Well, if you had anything to do with kidnapping him, then the reward is death," I warned.

He smiled again, but there was no humor behind it this time. "I had nothing to do with Hunter's disappearance. But I may know who did it."

"Who?" I demanded.

"Ah-ah-ah," he said, shaking his finger at me. "You first. What is my reward?"

"I'm not the king," I said. "I can't offer you any further reward. But you will have the gratitude of the entire kingdom."

"I think you can do better than that."

Frustrated, and afraid of the time he was wasting, I shook my head and promised him something I had no right to. "In addition to the spot on the King's Council, I'll give you anything else you want."

"Anything?"

"Anything within my power," I rushed out.

He nodded and slowly stood. "I have a feeling your power over the king is quite exceptional. You managed to marry the heir of the Manticore Kingdom, a human no less." He offered his hand to me. "Do we have a deal?"

I watched his steady hand and a feeling in the pit of my stomach told me not to shake it. *But what other choice did I have*? With no other leads, I had to make this deal with Alexander.

I raised my arm, but warning sirens blared in my head. I briefly closed my eyes, blocking them out, and shook Alexander's hand. "Deal," I said.

His smile spread across his face and nearly reached his ears. "Wonderful."

He turned and walked away to sit back down on the couch.

"Now, tell me how to get Hunter back," I insisted.

Alexander raised his eyes and looked at Anne. "Some of my men have been watching Pedersen. When Vivienne called just now, I followed up to see if there'd been any sighting of him."

"What are you implying?" asked Anne. "William had nothing to do with this. He was with Hunter when they took him."

My heart sank. Alexander didn't know where Hunter was. He was just making this up to get back at his rivals. I shook my head and prepared to leave when Alexander's voice stopped me.

"I wasn't talking about William or Mathias. My men followed Hans—your father-in-law."

Anne stood rigidly by my side. I reached for her hand and it was as cold as ice. I wasn't sure if I should believe Alexander's claims, but Anne's reaction told me there must be some truth in it.

"Have your men found Hans?" I asked.

Still looking at Anne, Alexander answered, "One of my men just called me saying they'd spotted him near the mountains."

"Which mountain range? Can your men take me there?" I pleaded.

"I can take you myself in the morning," Alexander said, leaning back on the couch.

Curling my hands into fists by my side, I scolded him, "I want to go now. I can't wait until morning. What if they...what if they hurt him before then."

"If they wanted to kill Hunter or Nicholas, they'd have done so already. But my hunch is they went to all this trouble to kidnap them for a reason."

"They want me," I said in a muffled voice, but knew Alexander heard me.

He leaned forward in his seat again. "And why is that?"

I shook my head, "I... I don't know why," I stammered. *Had they found out about me and my powers? Did they want me for themselves? Were they holding Hunter hostage, knowing I would finally come to them?*

Alexander studied my face for a few moments and said, "If it's you they want, then we need time to plan Hunter's release without getting you captured. And you, my little human, will need rest to execute this properly."

He was right. I wouldn't be able to do this with no sleep at all. "All right, what did you have in mind?"

Alexander smiled. "First, Anne must go back home and tell William and Mathias that you have no idea where Hunter is. I am certain this information will make its way back to Hans. If it is, in fact, you they want, they will seek you out and bring you to him."

"But why not just go straight there in the morning?"

"Because we do not know how many manticores are already inside the mountain. We may be outnumbered, and I'm not willing to risk it. No, we get them to believe you know nothing. Wait for them to make their move, but I will be behind you only a few minutes later. They won't be looking for us. They will believe you got there because they wanted you there, not because you had my help in finding their location. Do you understand?"

The plan was a bit murky, but I had nothing better to offer. "Fine. But if I don't hear from anyone by noon, then you will take me to that mountain range, even if I have to drag you there myself."

Alexander raked his gaze across my body and smiled.

"Looks can be deceiving, Alexander," I said. "I wouldn't underestimate me."

"On the contrary, my dear," he drawled. "I'm excited to see what you are capable of."

I needed to be careful around Alexander. He couldn't find out what I was. He was cunning and one of the most notorious manticores in Norway. He could never find out the truth about me.

"Call me as soon as you hear from Hans," said Alexander, writing his number on a piece of paper. "I will have my men ready to leave at once."

"What should I tell William?" asked Anne, wringing her hands.

"Nothing," I whispered, turning my back to Alexander and Vivienne. "The less he knows, the better."

"But if he found out that I knew you were going to attack his father..." worried Anne. "I can't hide that from him."

I pulled Anne closer to the door, hoping it was far enough away for Alexander not to hear. "Anne, I do not want to hurt William, but if he gets in my way of saving Hunter, I won't have a choice. For his safety, say nothing."

Anne looked at me, confusion lining her face. I knew she wondered how a human girl could hurt her much larger husband. "I have skills that make me very effective in handling manticores," I explained.

Anne shook her head, and said, "All right. But you have one day, that's it. Then I must tell him."

"Deal. One day. That's all I ask."

Anne nodded, and I turned to face Alexander. "All right. I will call you tomorrow." I walked over to pick up the piece of paper with his number. "You better be right about this."

"I'm shaking in my boots," he said.

I stared at him and whispered a chant underneath my breath. His hand jerked violently and he spilled his drink on the couch. "Shit," he shouted.

"You should be more careful. You almost spilled that on Vivienne."

He stared at me dumbfounded, but I just turned on my heels and left.

"Do you want me to take you back to our house?" Anne asked when she caught up to me.

I didn't feel comfortable with Mathias there and definitely didn't want to be there if Hans returned home.

"No, if you could take me back to my hotel, that would be great."

"I don't think you should be alone," she said.

"I'll be safe inside the hotel. They wouldn't try anything with so many witnesses inside. I think it's the best place for me right now. I just want to get some rest."

Anne pursed her lips but didn't argue further. She turned left and drove me back to the hotel. Despite having the two most important men in my life taken from me, I could no longer keep my eyes open. I stumbled into bed and drew the covers over me. I would get some sleep and be ready to battle the next day. One way or another, I would get Nicholas and Hunter back.

Nineteen

Michaela

The next morning, I quickly dressed and paced my hotel room, waiting for Alexander to meet me upstairs to go over the plan one more time. He'd called said he'd be here by nine o'clock. I looked down at my watch. It was only eight-thirty.

I debated if I should call my grandmother and get her advice, but I knew she would worry. There wasn't much she could do hundreds of miles away. It was best that she focused on Violet while I took care of my family here. Instead, I tried calling Hunter's phone again. It rang several times, but there was still no answer. Frustrated, I threw the phone. It hit the mattress, bounced up, and fell onto the ground. I would have just left it on the floor if it hadn't started ringing... *Oh my God, Hunter!* But when I reached for the phone, it wasn't his number that scrolled past my screen. It was Alexander's.

"I don't want to lead them to your room," he said. "Meet me inside the stairwell down the hall in five minutes."

"Have you seen anyone watching me?" I asked, looking out the window. Several cars zipped by, but no one stood around the entrance.

"I didn't. But that doesn't mean they're not there," he said, then ended the call.

Five minutes later, I put on my boots and walked down the hallway toward the stairs. I looked over my shoulder in case anyone was watching. When I didn't see any movement, I opened the door and nearly ran into Alexander.

"Did anyone follow you?" he asked, grabbing my shoulders and pulling me away from the door.

"No, I don't think so." I smoothed out my jacket.

"All right. Here's the plan. You're going to let yourself get kidnapped." He pointed his long finger at me.

I smacked it away. "Whoa, hold on. Why would I want to do that?"

"Because we have to let Pedersen think he's in control. We don't want his men suspicious and alert him that we're on our way."

I ran my fingers through my hair. His plan made sense.

"I'll follow at a distance with several manticores with me," he continued. "We'll meet you at the cave and help you get Hunter and Nicholas out."

I searched Alexander's eyes, looking for something that would help me trust him. His eyes held my stare.

"All right?"

No crinkles creased his eyes, no wink, no nothing. Only my gut telling me I had to go now. "All right."

"Good," he said with a sigh. He crossed his arms over his chest. "The only problem is, you'll have to get away from your captors before they drag you into the cave."

That wasn't a problem. "Leave that part to me."

He tilted his head. "You know, I get the feeling there's something really special about you."

I opened the door. "Yes, I'm desperate enough to walk into a trap."

"Well, let's hope you get there in time."

I stopped and turned around to face him. "What are you talking about?"

"We have a spy in Pedersen's camp," he explained, as though such an accomplishment were an everyday occurrence. Perhaps it was for Alexander Larsen. "He told us they're torturing Hunter and his body isn't healing as quickly as it should be. He must be exhausted."

"Let's go," I said and ran toward the elevator.

"I'll be right behind you."

I didn't turn around. I knew he didn't mean now, but in the car instead. I hoped we were right about Pedersen wanting me alive. Otherwise, I wasn't just walking into a trap, I was about to stand before a firing squad.

Pressing the elevator button for the lobby, I inhaled a deep breath as the mirrored doors closed.

I can do this. I would let them take me.

But when the elevator doors opened again, I hesitated. My legs were heavy and each step toward the front door felt as though it would be my last.

Stop being dramatic. I will be fine. I have to be. For Hunter, for Nicholas, and especially for Violet.

I saw them across the street from the hotel just as they laid eyes on me. They quickly averted their gaze, but it was too late. I may not have noticed if I hadn't expected them.

"Good morning," I said, pasting a smile on my face for the concierge as I walked past her desk. I pushed through the first set of doors and collected my nerves.

"Good morning, Ms. Durand," said the valet when I stepped outside. "Can I get a cab for you?"

"No, that's fine. I think I'll walk."

I pulled up the collar of my jacket and shoved my hands in the pockets. I took only three steps from the front door when I felt their eyes on me. Those tiny hairs on the back of my neck stood up. Despite my anticipation, fear still raced through my body. My legs wanted to run, but I held them back. My heart fluttered in my chest, but I breathed deeply to settle it. Finally, when I rounded the corner, away from the hotel, I heard footsteps behind me. A car screeched along the side of the road and a pair of hands grabbed me from behind.

I struggled against him. "Let me go."

Instinctively, I punched him in the face when he tried to pull me into the car. I guess I had learned something from all my lessons with Adam. Wiping the blood from his face, he pulled out a knife and held it against my throat.

"Don't kill her, you idiot," shouted the driver. "That's not part of the plan."

"Shut up," he yelled back.

I got the feeling he no longer cared about the plan. He pushed me inside the car and closed the door behind us.

"Drive," he yelled at his friend, who gunned the gas pedal. I tried to open the door, but it was locked, as I suspected. My captor pulled me toward him and I pounded, with both fists, on his chest. He let me go, only to snap his hand around my throat. Fear held me down tighter than his fingers did. I closed my eyes and prayed I would survive this.

When I didn't fight back, he squeezed harder, closing my passageway. Instinctively, knowing I would die if he didn't let up, I fought against his hold, raking my nails across his face, trying anything to stop him.

"Enough!" he shouted. He turned his head, looking out the window, probably assessing how far we were from the hotel by now. He must have been satisfied by the distance because he finally let me go. I coughed violently, my throat throbbing with the need for air. He sat back in his seat, as though he hadn't almost killed me. His slicked-back dark hair and beard shone in the afternoon light. He had blood on his face and shirt, but my scratches already looked to be healing.

Without looking my way, he said, "Sit back and get comfortable. It's going to be a long drive."

I narrowed my eyes at him, but he just grinned. "I thought that was going to be a lot harder than it actually was back there," he said.

I tilted my head. "Breaking your nose wasn't hard enough?"

He sucked his lips into his mouth and wiggled his nose a fraction. "There were rumors about you being some sort of manticore slayer. I guess he was wrong."

"Who?" I leaned forward to look him in the eye, but he kept staring straight ahead.

"You'll find out soon enough."

"You're taking me to him?" I asked, my pulse racing.

"Yes."

"Are Hunter and Nicholas there?"

He smiled. "The heir is there. I just don't know if he'll still be alive by the time we get there."

"I swear, if anything happens to Hunter, I will—"

He swung his head, his eyes hardened, and his lips curled. "You will what?"

I kept my mouth shut, not wanting to tell this manticore anything more than he needed to know.

He sneered. "That's what I thought."

I closed my eyes and counted to ten. Hunter said it helped him rein in his anger. Seven, six, five—but it wasn't working for me. I listened to their heartbeats and knew I could kill them at this moment if I wanted to.

Not yet though, not yet.

Twenty

Michaela

I peeked at the clock on the center console. It was nearly noon. More than two hours had passed since they had abducted me outside of the hotel. I had spied in the rearview mirror a car following us about thirty minutes into the ride, but the driver hadn't noticed. I glanced up at the mirror again now, but the car was gone. Lost in my thoughts, I didn't speak for most of the way up. I was too busy going over scenarios in my head and they were probably too busy congratulating themselves.

I thought up different possibilities on how I would get away from these guys when we arrived at the cave where they held Hunter. My chest tightened. Dropping my head, I prayed I'd still find him alive.

The breath and beauty of the mountain range flickered across the window, pulling me out of my miserable thoughts. The brown and green covered hills stood boldly against the blue sky. There were no clouds nor barriers from the sun's rays reaching down on us, their warmth suffocating in the car. I unzipped my jacket. The brute's eyes briefly glanced my way. But I frowned and shifted in my seat, moving further away from him. His eyes roamed from my face down to my breasts.

"What are you looking at?" I hissed.

When he smiled, I shook my head. "How unoriginal," I said. "Creepy villain leering at the girl."

"I don't have to be the villain here," he said. "The way you defended yourself back there was very attractive."

"I understand you manticores appreciate physical dominance, but I married a man who flexes his mind."

His smile broadened and he tilted his head lower. "We'll soon see about the married bit. You may be a widow after this."

I knew he was trying to rattle me, so I kept my face straight and maintained my composure, despite the turmoil raging inside my body. His words had hit their mark. My heart pounded in my chest and I recited a litany in my head: he's still alive, he's still alive, he's still alive. I raked my hair off my face and sat back further in the seat.

The car slowed down as we approached the mountain. There were several trees around us and I hadn't noticed the opening to the mountain until the driver parked the car in front. "We're here," he said.

"Get out of the car," ordered the brute beside me. I checked the mirrors but didn't see any other car around us. It didn't matter. I had to stick to the plan.

"I don't think so," I said and closed my eyes.

His fingers crept across my throat, but I still didn't move.

"I said, get out," he roared.

When I didn't move, he pressed the button on my seatbelt and released it, the strap recoiling back. The belt whipped past my chin.

"Move," he ordered again. This time, he put his hands on my shoulders and tried to pull me out of the car. His grip was strong, his fingers squeezed my flesh.

My lips moved effortlessly, reciting the words I had practiced many times before.

Vos es defessus. Dormies ad proximos duodecim horas. You are exhausted. Sleep for the next twelve hours.

His hands fell limply onto the backseat, then his body slumped down beside me. Placing two fingers to his throat, I checked his pulse. He was still alive, just sleeping, as I'd commanded.

I looked over at the driver's seat. The other manticore had fallen face-first onto the steering wheel. I leaned over to make sure he was all right too, but I didn't need to check his pulse, his snores were sign enough.

I stepped out of the car and surveyed the scene around me. I expected to find manticores standing outside, but the area was deserted. Trees and rocks surrounded me instead. The road led only to this mountain range, so there were no other cars for miles. It was quiet. Too quiet.

Where is he?

I walked away from the entrance, closer to the trees, and gasped when a figure appeared from behind one of them.

"My God, you scared me," I scolded him.

He shook the leaves off of his blond hair. "Sorry, I thought you saw me," he said, then whistled. Ten other men and women stepped out from behind trees and bushes.

"It looks as though our strategy worked," he said with a smile. "We're here and Pedersen thinks it's all because of him." Looking back at the car, he added, "And you managed not to get yourself dragged into the cave."

I smoothed the wrinkles from my jacket and returned his smile. "Did you doubt me, Alexander?" I asked.

"Only a bit, but you've proven yourself. I shouldn't have been surprised since you somehow convinced a manticore, the heir no less, to marry you."

"Hunter didn't marry me for my clever planning," I winked and he laughed.

"Are they dead?" he asked, flicking his head toward the car.

"No. But they won't bother us."

When he raised his eyebrow, I lied. "I knocked them out with a sleeper hold."

"Impressive."

"You manticores are easy to handle."

"Not all of us," he said and looked up at the opening in the mountain. "This is the place my men spotted Hans."

"How did you get here so fast?"

"We took a shortcut through the valley," he said, raking his gaze across the deserted terrain. "There's been no activity outside since we've arrived. But that may change soon since he's expecting you now. Seeing you here won't be a surprise to Hans, but my men and I will be." He raised his hand to wave his army over.

This was the part of my plan I was unsure about, especially how Alexander would react. "I need you and your men to stay out here," I told him.

"What are you talking about?" he asked, coming to a stop in front of a large boulder at the entrance, a hand on his hip. "I brought my men so we can help you save Hunter, as we discussed. You said I would be rewarded if Hunter was returned to you." He pointed a finger at me. "This better not be you backtracking from your word?" he growled.

"It's not," I assured him, raising my hands in front of me. "You've brought me this far and I will keep my word. But I have to go in there alone. What I need to do is dangerous and I don't want you or your army in there."

He walked toward me until his face was only inches from mine. "We are not afraid of danger, Michaela. We thrive on it."

I knew this would be the hardest part, so I pressed on. "If you want your reward, promise me you will stay out here. No matter what you hear inside, no matter who tries to escape or come into the mountain. You stay out. Do you understand me?"

A soft growl rumbled in his chest, his eyes shifting across my body. "You are not bringing any weapons?"

"I have a knife in my boot."

"One knife against a mountain full of manticores?"

My eyes glanced to the side toward the people behind him, then returned to Alexander's inquisitive gaze. "Yes." I didn't flinch.

"Fine. We'll do it your way," he said, taking a step back, allowing me to pass.

When I nearly reached the cave's entrance, Alexander called me back. "Michaela?"

I turned to look at him over my shoulder. "Yes?"

"Don't get yourself killed. You owe me and I intend to cash in." His stare held me until a smile crept over his face.

I rolled my eyes. "Your concern is touching," I said.

Then I squared my shoulders and walked into the lion's den.

Twenty-One

Michaela

The entrance was half-hidden by a large boulder from the inside and the outside. As I walked through, it surprised me to find no guards waiting for me. The ground and walls of the cave were a deep brown with jagged edges all along the walls. Despite the smell of fresh earth, the ground was dry and dusty. I stood at the entrance and listened. Nothing but the wind rustling the leaves in the trees behind me, so I continued.

After a few brief steps into the tunnel, the rays from the sun receded, and I had to pull out the small flashlight I'd brought with me. The narrow light only illuminated the path in front of me. I was blind to almost everything around me. I never particularly hated the dark, but I didn't enjoy walking into a situation without knowing what to expect. I relied on my ears to warn me of any danger as I slowly walked deeper into the cave.

When my jacket pocket started vibrating, I nearly jumped out of my skin. I unzipped the pocket and pulled out my phone. A number flashed on the screen. *Now's not a good time, Astrid.*

I continued walking along the dirt path. *Buzz.*

I'm just going to shut it off.

I yanked out my phone again to do just that and saw the text message from Astrid:

It's Larsen. I just saw security footage of him with the two victims at the bar the night of the murders, minutes before the victims were killed.

I looked back toward the entrance of the cave, where Alexander stood only moments ago. He had helped me form this plan.

A sound—a rock falling—caught my attention to my left. I stood still, listening for any other movement. Nothing. I took another step forward and someone grabbed me from behind. Dropping the light, I kicked and elbowed my attacker. He grunted and let go.

"*Bitch!*" he cried.

Another pair of hands, this time from my right, grabbed my waist and lifted me off the ground. I tried to kick but couldn't reach him. Someone pulled my hair from behind, lifting my chin to the ceiling. Gasping, I prepared a chant to stop him from slitting my throat when he wrapped a blindfold across my eyes instead. He set me down on my feet and I wobbled for only a moment until I regained my balance and caught my breath.

"You're lucky I have instructions to keep you alive," someone whispered in my ear. It was the one who had sworn at me earlier.

"You're lucky you're not holding me down anymore or you'd be dead already," I told him.

He grabbed my arm and shoved me forward. With the blindfold, I couldn't see anything and unfortunately relied on his pushes to lead me in the right direction.

"Where are Morris and Leonard?" asked the grumpy one, shoving me.

"I didn't see them, just her," the other responded.

Morris and Leonard must have been the manticores that brought me here. I spoke up. "They told me to walk into the cave alone. Said something about planning to wait in the car in case anyone came from the outside."

The grumpy one grunted and mumbled, "Lazy bastards," under his breath.

We walked for several minutes. My arm would certainly have a bruise from him tomorrow. Finally, he pulled my shoulder back to stop me. The air felt colder here. I figured we were quite deep inside the mountain now. A chill ran down my spine.

"Michaela!" Nicholas shouted.

And just like that, relief washed over me and my knees weakened at the sound of his voice. "Nicholas! Thank God, you're okay."

The guard pushed me against a wall. "Wait here," he said and walked away. When I tried to pull my blindfold off, the other manticore slapped my hand. I gritted my teeth but kept my mouth shut.

"Nicholas, are you hurt?" I asked.

"Only my pride," he said. "Michaela, there's something I have to tell you. The manticore who kidnapped me, it was—"

Footsteps crunched against the dirt floor and stopped in front of me.

"Hello, Michaela," said a voice a few feet in front. "It's good to see you."

"Unfortunately, I cannot say the same about you." I pointed to my blindfold.

His voice grew closer to me. "I heard your eyes can inflict pain upon us."

I held back my surprise and my smile. Shocked to learn that he knew about my powers, I also realized he had misinterpreted the information he was given. *But who could have told him?*

"You have me at a disadvantage," I said. "Who are you and what do you want?"

By getting him to talk, I hoped to figure out where he held Hunter. Then, I could finally end all of this.

"I want my son back," he whispered.

I hadn't expected that response. "Who's your son?"

His footsteps grew closer and I wet my lips, preparing to chant if needed.

"She probably didn't even know his name," he said.

"Who? What are you talking about?"

"Don't lie, Michaela!" he shouted, and I flinched. "How could you not know? She must have taught you everything."

The cold blade of a knife pressed against my cheek. I couldn't think straight. I tried to process his words, but my thoughts were stuck on getting us out of this place in one piece. I couldn't care less about the motives of a madman. I just needed to know where to find Hunter.

"If it's me you want, then let Hunter and Nicholas go."

"I can't do that. They know too much."

He ran the flat of the knife down my face, resting the tip on my throat. He pressed it deeper and my breath hitched. I whispered a chant that made him believe he had no feeling in his hand. The knife instantly dropped to the ground.

"Are you all right, boss?" the guard asked.

"I'm fine," he said and cleared his throat. "It's time to bring her to the altar."

"Yes, boss."

Footsteps approached me, then a hand grabbed my shoulder. I cringed from a shot of pain. My flesh tender from his earlier roughness.

Someone opened a door and the slow creak felt like ants crawling over my body.

"Come on," the guard said and pushed me forward. Blindfolded, I took a tentative step, tapping the ground in front of me, then another, worried he would push me into a cell or hole. He shoved harder, and I fell onto the dirty ground.

"Michaela!" a hoarse voice shouted in front of me.

Hunter!

"You're still alive!" I shouted. Tears caught inside the blindfold and wet the back of my eyes. The guard held me down, stopping me from wiping them away. Hearing his voice overwhelmed me. I'd been so worried but had needed to keep my composure to formulate a plan. Having found Hunter, I lost my control and cried in earnest.

"He's still alive, for now," said the man. "Bring down her blindfold. But only for a minute and stay away from her gaze," He ordered the guards.

When he pulled the fabric down, I recoiled from the vision before me. Hunter's dark hair splattered across his face, smeared with blood, and sweat. They had tied his hands and feet to a wooden table that looked to be hundreds of years old; the ropes cutting into his skin, leaving open angry red wounds. I worried they were already infected. His beautiful body was tarnished with bruises, along his ribcage, sides, and arms.

"Michaela, look at me," he said.

My God, how could I not!

My eyes roamed across his flesh, tallying all his injuries, and wondering which one was most fatal. My chants alone couldn't heal his body. I needed to put my hands on his wounds as well. I had to get to him, touch him, so my powers would heal him. I pulled against the guards, both held me down now, but they didn't budge.

"Michaela, look at me. Focus," Hunter said again. "Look me in the eye."

I did, and the pain in his eyes nearly brought me to my knees. "Oh, Hunter," I whispered.

His eyes pleaded with mine, and his face hardened. "Don't waste any more time," he said. "Get yourself away from here, now. Go!"

"I'm not leaving without you," I said, shaking my head. *How could he even think that?*

"They know about you. They know everything," he cried. "She told them. You must leave. Think of Violet."

Violet. The mention of her name tore me from the inside. But I would never forgive myself if I left Hunter. Never. "I am thinking of Violet," I whispered. "Always." A movement to my left caught my attention. I turned toward the man barking the orders.

Hans!

It was Hans Pedersen all along. My heart broke, knowing how this news would devastate Anne and William.

A man, using a walking stick, strode into the room. "Is this the girl?"

"Get out of here, Larsen!" shouted Hans.

Larsen.

"I'm leaving. I just wanted to see her before it's too late," he said, standing dangerously close to me. "After the sacrifice, there won't be any others like her."

Larsen was short, only an inch taller than me, with a shock of white hair and a full white beard.

"Which Larsen are you?" I asked.

"I'm the mayor of Oslo, Glen Larsen." He smiled, but his fangs were out and I took a step back. "Don't worry, darling. I won't hurt you."

I recalled Vivienne mentioning Glen Larsen when she recounted the influential families in Norway. Wasn't he Alexander's uncle? Why hadn't Alexander mentioned him or his involvement?

"Larsen," Hunter growled, his head turned to the side, his eyes pleading with the man before me. "It's not too late for you. Get her out of here and I won't kill you."

Larsen chuckled. "Why would I do that when I went through all the trouble of luring that police officer and woman to Pedersen? No, we have a deal. He gets his justice and I get a path cleared to the Prime Minister's Office."

Power. This was all about power for Larsen. But it was personal for Pedersen. I just didn't know what he wanted from me yet.

Larsen was so focused on me he hadn't heard the footsteps behind him, or perhaps he hadn't thought to worry about them. But the next second, Hans wrapped his hands around Larsen's head and snapped his neck. I screamed and covered my face with my hands.

"No!" shouted Hunter. "You're fucking crazy, Pedersen. You know that?"

Pedersen stepped away from the body, and Glen fell at his feet. He walked toward Hunter. "I'm not crazy," he said. "I could not let that man become Prime Minister and hold this over me for the rest of my life. No. He served his purpose. The police will figure out that he was the one who met with the victims. It won't be long until they accuse him of the murders while I'm on a road trip in the mountains."

"What about Astrid? She knows the truth," said Hunter.

"You think I'm worried about one more casualty?"

"My father won't believe you."

"There's no evidence, Hunter. He will only have suspicions."

I thought of Vivienne and Nicholas. He would kill them too for knowing too much.

"Let him go!" I shouted and pierced Hans with my stare. "Now!"

"Cover her eyes. Do it!" he shouted, pointing his finger at me. The guards immediately pulled up the blindfold and darkness engulfed me once more. It wasn't enough to stop me, though, and I would make these guards and Hans pay for every injury they had caused us.

I concentrated on the manticore's heartbeats next to me. In my head, I told the guards, with all of their strength, to hold down Pedersen instead of me. Immediately, the manticores pinning me down let go and rushed past me.

"What are you doing, you fools?" shouted Pedersen.

I pulled the blindfold from my eyes and ensured the chant had worked. The guards held Pedersen against the wall. I rushed to Hunter's side and placed my palms on his taunt chest. His heat radiated through me. I felt his strong heartbeat beneath my hands and chanted the words that would heal him. Each syllable rolled off my tongue like a powerful panacea.

"Hurry. We don't have much time," he whispered.

I nodded but placed my hands on his wrists instead to remove the ropes. As I worked, I repeated the words of the protection chant I had used in the battle against Elenora. It had saved Hunter then. I prayed it would work this time, too. When his arms and legs were finally free, he jumped off the table. "Let's go," he said and grabbed my hand.

"You won't get very far," said Pedersen, peering down the large room toward the exit. He struggled against the guards holding him back, but it was hopeless. "My men are just outside those doors. They have instructions to kill you on sight if you leave this room without me. If you open that door, I still get what I want."

Twenty-Two

Michaela

Pedersen's words hit me as I ran toward the door. I slammed into Hunter when he abruptly came to a halt. With a snarl on his face, he turned to Pedersen. "Call off your dogs," he demanded.

"And why would I do that?" he grinned. "You may have this mut holding me back but once you open that door, my men will tear you apart."

"Michaela, release the guards from your chant," said Hunter. "Pedersen and I will finish this."

"If this guard lets me go, I will kill her," growled Pedersen.

"Not if I get to you first," Hunter snarled back.

"I still don't understand," I turned to Hans. "Why do you hate me so much? I've never met you or your son."

"Shut up, Pedersen!" Hunter shouted. "Don't say a word!"

When Pedersen opened his mouth to speak, Hunter reached him in two strides and swung his fist. It connected with Pedersen's mouth and blood spewed against the wall. "I said, keep your mouth shut."

Pedersen's smile spread across his face, blood dripping from his teeth. He turned toward me and said, "You really don't know?"

When I didn't respond, he shook his head, then glared at me. "Your mother killed my son."

What? "My mother killed Erik?" I repeated aloud, refusing to believe but realizing it must be true. My mother was a manticore slayer and had come to Norway on a mission. The dots finally connected. I knew nothing of my mother's missions, so felt no guilt for her sins.

"I'm not proud of the things my mother did," I said, taking a step closer to Hans. "I'm sorry about your son, but that has nothing to do with me."

"But it does," he whispered. "When Elenora told me about you and your mother, I was angry. If your mother had stood before me at that moment, I would have broken her neck. But even if I'd killed her, it wouldn't have brought my son back. I thought nothing would until my dream. When the goddess Hel offered to return Erik to me, for a price, I took it. Your lifeblood for his soul."

"I know nothing about this goddess Hel, but your son is not coming back. Not if it means giving up my life. You know what I am capable of, Pedersen. It's over. Now call off your guards and we will take you before the king to stand trial for your actions. He may show mercy if you let us go now."

"You think I'll let you just walk out of here?"

"Yes," I told him.

"I won't ever give up on my family. Once this spell you have on these manticores wears off, I will come after you again."

"I'll be ready," I shot back, keeping my nerves strong, hoping I didn't show any of the fear I felt at his words. Hunter glared at Pedersen, but I grabbed his arm and pulled him with me toward the door.

Hans pursed his lips, his face trembling from the effort to contain his anger. His amber eyes burned with a fire behind them. "No. This ends today." Craning his neck, he shouted, "Guards!"

The doors flung open, and I counted about twenty manticores, at least from what I could see down the dark tunnel. I thanked God I had said the protection chant over Hunter because I needed to work fast. I couldn't pick manticores individually now, so I inhaled a deep breath in, my chest rising alongside my lungs, and I repeated the words—the plan I had formulated back in the car.

Manticores noctis. Vocem meam audi. Tutus non es. Non ab aliquo. Pugna pro vita tua. Frater tuus non est amicus tuus sed inimicus tuus. Hostem nunc interfice. The words swirled in my mind, reverberating back to me: *Manticores of the night. Hear my voice. You are not safe. Not from anyone. Fight for your life. Your brother is not your friend, but your foe. Kill your enemy now.*

The raging crowd of manticores running toward us halted. Their stern faces and angry fists held in place, and all at once, they turned and looked at each other. It was only for an instant before the battle erupted. Roars and growls bounced off the cavernous walls, echoing in my ears. I thought I could get used to the sound, but my hands flew to cover them. "Wait here and try to stay out of the way as much as you can," Hunter said.

"Where are you going?" He couldn't possibly be thinking of fighting in his condition.

"I'm not leaving until I've settled a score," he growled. "The big one is mine!" He jumped over a guard and pushed another out of his way outside the doors until he reached what looked to be a mountain of a man.

Dear Lord, he's gone insane!

I weaved my way through the crowd until I reached them.

Hunter punched the man in the gut and kicked both of his knees until the guard fell to the ground. In a swift movement, the giant jumped back onto his feet and landed a hit to Hunter's bruised ribs. When he didn't shout out in pain, confusion crossed the giant's face. I let out a breath. *The protection chant had worked.*

Hunter rallied back with a kick to the man's chest. He fell backward, his tall frame taking two other manticores down with him. I looked around. Bodies lay on the ground, some whimpering, others laying frightfully still. Small battles continued among the fighters, but Hunter and I would not stick around to find out how those ended. "Let's get out of here," I said.

"No."

Surprised, I turned back around to gawk at him.

"I'm not leaving without taking care of Pedersen," he said.

"Hunter, don't do it. It's not worth it."

"Yes, it is. Sleeping soundly each night after today. Not having to worry about someone coming after you or Violet is worth it. It is worth everything to me."

I couldn't blame him. It sounded wonderful to me too, but not at the expense of killing someone. But I could see it in Hunter's eyes that he felt differently. "I can't watch," I said.

"Then go," he whispered, but before I could walk away, he pulled me back and into his arms. He kissed me until my lungs burned for air. I gasped when he pulled his lips away. He turned, but I grabbed his hand. I threw myself at him again, wrapping my arms around his waist.

"Come back to me," I whispered.

He nodded, and I let him go. I watched him stride back into the room where they'd kept him prisoner. I turned and fled down the hallway. "Nicholas!" I shouted.

I found him tied up, sitting on the ground. Dirt stained his white shirt. I loosened the knot. Nicholas twisted his hands through the small opening and the rope fell to the ground. He pulled me into his arms.

"Are you all right?" he asked, patting my shoulders, and looking for injuries.

"I'm okay. Let's get you out of here." I ran toward the entrance of the cave, a stream of light guiding us in the right direction. I cupped my hand over my eyes when we reached outside, the sun blinding me momentarily. "Go, hide yourself in the trees." I pointed toward the woods. "I'm going back for Hunter."

"Michaela—" he argued.

"Go!" I shouted, and he stumbled but ran into the forest.

I turned to go back inside when a movement caught my attention. The figure was small, wore black trousers and a black blouse, her long hair streaming behind her as she ran—*Elenora*! *Oh no, no, no*! She would not leave this cave without facing the consequences of her actions.

"Elenora!" I shouted, and she turned around. Her grin disgusted me. I raced after her, but she ran toward the trees. She stumbled on the uneven ground and I caught up to her. I grabbed her long hair and yanked her back as hard as I could.

"Ow!" she screamed and turned to slap me across the face. My hand instinctively rose to my cheek, and my skin burned from her fury.

"You're the one who told them about my mother and me," I shouted.

She tried to run, but I grabbed her blouse.

"You're not leaving here," I yelled.

"Your powers don't work on me anymore, sweetheart. You made sure of that when you took mine away."

"You still found a way to save yourself. How did you escape just now?"

She struggled against my hold. Testing my strength. "When the battle erupted, I ran."

Like a rat, Elenora knew when to run away from danger. I would not let her run very far. "This needs to stop. You need to stop hurting me and my family."

"I will never stop, Michaela. You've taken everything from me—everything!" she shouted.

"You did that to yourself," I shouted back.

She took two steps forward and got right in my face. "You took my instincts, my place in the kingdom, and even my family. I won't stop until I take yours."

An image of Violet popped in my head and panic like I'd never experienced before strangled my veins. Elenora wouldn't stop until she destroyed it all and I couldn't let that happen.

Her lips turned up. "You finally get it, don't you?" she said.

I nodded. "I do."

She reached for my throat, and I slapped her hand away. She came at me from the other side, but I blocked that too. I didn't see her forehead coming, though, until she slammed it into my face. Pain blinded me for a moment and I staggered back. Elenora pushed me to the ground. I shook my head and while the world appeared blue and fuzzy; I saw her foot just above my face. Grabbing her ankle, I yanked her down onto the ground. I clamored to my knees and straddled her. Wrapping my hands around her neck, I said, "Promise me you'll walk away and never come back."

She shook her head, and I squeezed my fingers. "Promise me!" I shouted. She spat in my face. Instinctively, I wiped the spit away with my hand. She pushed me and heaved herself on top of me, latching her fingers around my throat. Where I had held back, Elenora did not. I could feel the air trapped in my windpipe between her hands and the edges of my vision blurred.

I tried to reach for the knife in my boot, but her body sat rigidly on top of mine. I couldn't move. In one quick motion, just like Adam had taught me, I heaved my hips up at the same time that I pulled her arms apart. The movement pushed her forward, slamming her head onto the hard ground. She grunted but still got up. I pulled out the knife from my boot and waved it in front of her. "Say it," I demanded. "Say you will leave us alone and never come back."

"I would rather die."

I put my shoulder down and ran toward her, ramming her body up against the boulder at the entrance of the cave. I placed my knife underneath her throat and steeled my voice until I felt confident it would not tremble. "Don't make me do this," I said with a steady voice, but my hand trembled instead. I felt sick to my stomach, knowing this was the only way I would finally be rid of Elenora in my life and Violet would be safe. I pushed the knife closer, cutting her flesh, and blood seeped down her neck. My hand shook, tremors wracked my body. I couldn't do it. I couldn't bring myself to end her life with my own bare hands.

I dropped the knife. The clang sounded like a gunshot, and we both jumped.

"I'm taking you back to the kingdom and locking you up," I said, taking a step back from her.

I turned to call out Alexander's name. I squinted but didn't see him anywhere.

"You will never be a worthy leader if you cannot finish your battles," said Elenora. She held the knife I had dropped only moments ago. I moved back, my hands up in surrender, and tried a chant to stop her heart. The words poured out of my mouth smoothly, but they had little effect on her. She stumbled for only a moment, clutching her chest with her other hand, but kept walking.

She fought back pain, but the chant wasn't enough to stop her.

Nicholas had warned me that my powers were not as effective on humans. I ran toward the woods, looking for something sharp or heavy to use as a weapon. I frantically looked around, but nothing but dried leaves were at my feet.

When her eyes looked past me and she smiled, I instinctively turned back, too. A river raged behind me. With nowhere else to go, I planted my feet and prepared to fight for my life. She came at me with the knife and I held her arm back. Being taller and stronger, she overpowered me, and I fell to one knee.

The knife inched closer to my face as she angled it down toward my heart. Sweat dripped from my forehead and back, using every muscle in my body to hold the blade away. But I was losing the fight.

The sharp tip easily went through my cotton fabric and pierced the skin on my chest. A dot of blood formed on the white T-shirt, but I jerked my head up and focused on pulling her away. My sweaty hands shook, and the blade went deeper.

A loud shriek rang in my ears and my eyes flew open. Elenora's eyes were round and as large as an owl's. She opened her mouth, forming an 'O'. Her body stood rigidly until it collapsed forward and would have landed on top of me if I didn't push the knife and her body away. Standing before me, brandishing a knife of his own, was Alexander.

"When you dropped the knife, I knew you would never kill her. So, I waited until the last second to give you a chance to fight her, but it looked like it wasn't going well for you. Hope you don't mind."

I shook my head emphatically. "No, not at all."

He stuck his hand out toward me, and I gladly took it. He pulled me up so I could stand, but my legs were still shaking.

"I thought I was going to die."

"Yeah, I thought so, too," he said. "I couldn't let that happen, you know. You're the only one who can fulfill my last reward."

I squeaked out a laugh and it sounded a bit hysterical even to my own ears.

"Where's Nicholas?" I asked.

"He's with my men."

I stood there for a few minutes, catching my breath, sucking in precious, life-giving air, then I put both my hands on his chest and shoved him as hard as I could. He stumbled backward.

"What was that for?"

"You lied to us! Your uncle was there. He was part of this whole plan. How do I know you won't slit my throat now?"

"If I wanted you dead, I would have let Elenora do it."

"Then why didn't you tell us?"

"I led you to the killer, didn't I? That's all that you needed to know."

"You played us!"

"I didn't play you. I merely guided you to where you needed to be, with the information you needed to get there."

"I don't like you," I said.

"You don't need to like me," he said and got closer to me. "But you do need to pay me my reward."

His eyebrows and lips formed a straight line, and I knew he wasn't kidding. He may have saved my life, but Alexander Larsen's actions weren't selfless.

I turned toward the entrance of the cave. Hunter still hadn't come out. If Alexander was willing to save my life for his reward, then I'd bet he'd be willing to save Hunter's, too.

"Come with me. Hunter may need our help," I said to Alexander.

"Oh, now I'm permitted to enter, your highness?" he said.

"Don't start," I warned him.

We entered the dark cave, and it was eerily quiet. As we got closer to the room where they had held Hunter, we found more bodies lying on the ground.

"Is that *The Mammoth*?" asked Alexander as we passed the hulk of the man Hunter had fought earlier. I shrugged my shoulders, unsure if that was his name. When I approached the doors to the room, I inhaled a sharp breath and prepared myself for what I would find on the other side. No sound came from inside. The battle was over there, too. I prayed I would find Hunter alive.

As I slowly pushed the doors open, I saw him. He was sweaty, bloody, but wonderfully alive. I ran to him. "Oh Hunter, I'm so glad you're okay." I stepped to wrap my arms around him, but he stopped me with a hand to my shoulder and looked down at my chest. He placed his other hand on the bloodstain next to my heart. I curled my hand on top of his. "I'm fine. Alexander saved me."

Hunter looked up and spotted Alexander. "Thank you," he said, his voice hoarse.

"I sort of killed your aunt in the process, though." Alexander shrugged his shoulders.

"Then I thank you twice."

Alexander smirked at that.

I looked down and saw Hans Pedersen's body on the ground. His head was angled in an awkward position and blood covered most of his grey suit, especially at his chest. Hunter pulled me into his arms. His body trembled and his chest rose, taking in a large breath.

"I could not let him get away with it," he whispered next to my ear.

I nodded and wrapped my arms around him. I noticed Alexander turn over his uncle's body but did not say a word.

"Let's get out of here," said Hunter, and kept his arms around my waist as we left the cold, lifeless cave.

Twenty-Three

Hunter

Alexander drove Michaela and me back to my hotel. He mentioned something about a reward, but I was too tired to listen. My body throbbed everywhere, my nerves were shot and my mind was foggy from the constant worry of what would happen to Michaela. Now that she was safe, and the adrenaline seeped from my veins, I felt spent.

I didn't tell her what happened between Pedersen and me. She didn't need to hear the graphic details of how I slowly tore apart his muscles from each one of his limbs, as he had done to mine. Nor how I enjoyed it when I held him against the wall by the throat with one hand while I pushed my claws deep inside his rib cage. When they pierced his heart, I clenched my fist tighter. When the bloodlust raged and the anger of what he had put us through stormed through my body, I was truly a monster. I pushed the images and instincts back where I had carefully hidden them before, deep within my soul.

I barely recalled entering the elevator. I simply dropped my head back and closed my eyes. When the elevator binged, I moved my body only when Michaela steered me out and into the hallway. Once inside the hotel room, she guided me toward the bed. I was about to throw myself back onto the mattress when she stopped me. "Your clothes are filthy. Let me take them off so I can see where you're injured." Her eyes assessed my body. "There may be deep cuts or bruises that I missed in the cave."

I simply nodded, too exhausted and hurt to argue. Grasping the material at my waist, Michaela pulled my shirt from inside my pants, her fingers reaching underneath the hem to gather the material.

Her fingers grazed my stomach muscles. Her cool touch was like a balm on my burning flesh. I raised my arms, and she pulled up the shirt until it stretched over my head. Her eyes roamed my chest, her hand hovering above my heart. Goosebumps rose on my skin, anticipating her touch.

She gently placed her palm over my ribs, her smooth skin contrasting with the ugly purple bruises beneath them. I sucked in a breath, not from pain but the coolness of her touch.

"Don't move," she whispered, and I fought against exhaustion to hold myself still.

The iciness from her fingertips seeped deep within my skin until I felt their chill from inside my body. I watched as her hand rubbed at the bruise, erasing its ugly stain. Amazed, I looked up into her eyes, but she held them closed.

Her lips moved, and her breath rushed out. Without thinking, I bent my head down to kiss her, and she gasped, taking my breath away. I smiled, and she returned it with a grin of her own.

"I told you to hold still," she chuckled.

"I couldn't help myself," I argued back.

She closed her eyes once more and resumed chanting. Her hand moved to the other side of my chest, cooling the ribs there. I sucked in a deep breath, finally able to fill my lungs to capacity, and let it out.

"Good," she murmured.

"It feels so good," I whispered back.

She smirked, then moved her hand toward my back, where *The*

Mammoth had kicked my kidneys. I flinched and sucked back a groan, but she kept her hand steady. I was glad I no longer had to worry about him. She moved her hand onto my other side, and I lost sight of her when she stood behind me. I felt her, though.

Her hands roamed my back, healing any wounds she found. I breathed deeply once more, feeling no pain or puncture when I inhaled. It was as though a new energy coiled within me, not hot or burning, but cool and ethereal. My feverish exhaustion gave way to an awakening of untapped cells within my body. I felt stronger and lighter at the same time.

"Take off your pants," she said.

My eyes flew open. "You read my mind," I said.

She laughed again. "Easy, tiger. I need to check for wounds on your legs and feet."

Regardless of her reasons, I shucked off my pants and waited for her examination. She ran her hands along my thighs, cupping my muscles, my knee, and finally my calf. I ground my teeth when her fingers landed on the open wounds at my ankles caused by the coarse ropes.

"These look infected," she said, then stood to examine my wrists. Those cuts looked red and angry, too. Gently, she ran her fingers down my arms and bent down to do the same to my legs.

I looked up at the ceiling, concentrating on the blood rushing to my extremities. All of my extremities. The frigidness of her touch did not cool down the rest of me. In fact, a new fever took over, and I grabbed her wrists and pulled her up in front of me. Her brow creased. "Are you all right? Does something else hurt?"

I nodded and raised my eyebrows. She slapped my shoulder and tried to walk away, but my hand circled her waist and pulled her back to my front. Wrapping my arm across her middle, I dropped my head to her ear and whispered, "I thought I'd never see you again."

She squeezed my arm and pulled me in tighter. "I would never let that happen."

Closing my eyes, I smiled. This strong, beautiful woman was my wife. A growl slipped from my lips. The instinct to possess her overtook me, and I leaned down once more.

"I want you," I whispered. Then placed my lips onto her neck and kissed my way down until I reached the spot where her neck met her shoulder. She moaned in pleasure. The sweetest sound I'd ever heard. My body hummed. I ran my hands down her front and cupped her breasts. She inhaled deeply, her flesh spilling out of my palms. I pulled her in closer and she raised her arms above her head, reaching to hold my nape.

Watching her body open to me snapped the last bit of my control. With a growl, I placed one arm under her neck and the other behind her knees and lifted her like a princess, even though she had rescued me. I was about to show her how much I appreciated it.

I placed her head on the pillow and crawled up beside her. She stared at me with those violet eyes and I forgot my own name.

Only when her hands inched toward her blouse and unbuttoned her shirt did I move into action. I unbuttoned the last two, then pulled down her jeans. I'd seen her body—tasted her—hundreds of times, yet each time the sight of her still brought me to my knees.

My hands worshipped her body, and my mouth left a trail of goosebumps wherever it kissed. She panted and squirmed underneath me until she finally grabbed my face and pulled it up to hers. She raised her hips, curving her bare softness around me. Shutting my eyes on a hiss, I plunged into her.

She gasped, her back arching, her head falling back. I kissed her exposed neck and rocked within her, moving slowly at first, then when her hips spurred me on, I quickened my pace to meet her demands. I smiled when a groan escaped her lips and kept my movements steady when her breaths confirmed I was where I needed to be.

When her breathing quickened, I used my newfound strength to sharpen her pleasure until she finally cried out. Her fingers pulled me down and I surrendered. Spent, I fell next to her on the bed and pulled her languid body next to mine.

I smiled, as she was the one who looked utterly exhausted now. I held her until her breathing slowed and she fell asleep in my arms.

Twenty-Four

Michaela

I awoke in Hunter's arms, smiling and replete. He slept soundly beside me. I carefully lifted the comforter from my body and tiptoed toward my purse. Pulling out my phone, I placed a video call to my grandmother. She answered immediately, holding Violet in her arms. Seeing her bright eyes on my screen brought tears to my own, and I wiped them away before my grandmother noticed.

"Is everything all right, Michaela? Why are you crying?" she asked. I guess I hadn't wiped them fast enough.

"I'm fine, *Nonna*," I sniffed. No longer holding back my emotions. "Just happy to see you and Violet." At the sound of her name, Violet squealed, reached for the phone, bouncing against my grandmother's hip.

"Is that Violet?" a groggy voice asked behind me.

I turned to him. "Yes. Do you want to speak to her?"

I walked over to the bed and sat next to Hunter, who pulled himself up, his bareback against the headboard.

"How's my baby girl?" he crooned, grabbing the phone from my hand. I smiled at the crinkles around his eyes and shook my head.

"She's great," my grandmother said, bussing a kiss onto Violet's cheek. "How's everything in Norway?"

Hunter looked at me and I nodded, letting him know he could be honest with my grandmother. "Everything is fine. We caught the killer and should head home soon. Maybe even tomorrow."

"That's wonderful news," my grandmother cried. "Violet and I will be so happy to see you both at home."

I pulled the phone back from Hunter and blew Violet and my grandmother a kiss. "See you both very soon. Love you."

"Say goodbye, Violetta," my grandmother urged.

Violet waved, "Babababa," she babbled.

"Oh, she said goodbye." I sniffed. "Did I just miss her first word?"

Hunter shook his head. "No," he laughed. "Stop worrying. You will be with her before she learns to read."

Before I put my phone away, I dialed Nicholas's number. Last night, we dropped him off at his hotel. I didn't want to leave, but he assured me he was fine. More like ordering me to leave him alone. But I needed to hear his voice right now.

"Who are you calling now?" asked Hunter.

Nicholas, I mouthed.

"Hello?" Nicholas's voice rang clear on the other end.

"Hey, Nicholas. How are you feeling?" I breathed a sigh of relief.

"I'm all right, barely a scratch on me. How's Hunter?"

"He's fine." I paused, gathering my nerve to say the rest. "I'm so sorry, Nicholas."

"For what?"

"For getting you into this mess."

"Don't apologize. You're family, and I love you as if you were my own. I would run to hell and back for you."

I smiled at his words, despite the water gathering in my eyes. "I love you, too."

After arranging to see each other later, I ended the call. Turning toward the bathroom door, I caught a glimpse of Hunter stepping out of the shower. His toned muscles and tanned skin were free of any cuts or bruises, making me smile.

"Will you be ready to leave soon?" he asked, slinging a towel over his hips.

I bit my lip. "Yup. Just need to take a shower first myself."

"Okay, great. I want to leave for the Pedersen mansion soon."

I walked up to him, leaning against the bathroom door. "So soon?"

"We need to explain everything to William and Anne face to face," he said.

I nodded, but my stomach twisted into a knot. I pressed my fist against it. I worried about what William and Anne would say. *Would they hate us? Or would they understand?*

By the time Hunter pulled into the Pedersen's long driveway, it was already past noon. "Maybe we should come back later, in case they're having lunch."

"We can't put it off any longer," he said and turned off the engine. I reluctantly climbed out of the car. Hunter was by my side and held my hand as we crossed the stone walkway to the front door. I inhaled a sharp breath and slowly let it out.

The same older woman with her hair neatly tied back in a bun opened the door. "Are William and Anne at home?" asked Hunter.

"Please come in," she said, opening the door wider. "I'll see if they are taking visitors. We'll be serving lunch soon."

I shot Hunter an 'I told you so' glare with my eyebrow raised and he just grinned. It wasn't enough to put me at ease, though. The tapping of Anne's heels down the hallway alerted us before I saw them both turn the corner. William held Anne's hand, but his face didn't have the same friendly smile as the last time he greeted us at the door.

"Michaela, Hunter. I'm glad to see you're all right," he said. His concern twisted the knot in my stomach tighter. "Anne told me you'd gone in search of my father and there may be trouble. He didn't return last night, but he hadn't been back home for a couple of days now. Did you find him?"

I glanced at Anne. Her eyes met mine and she read the plea in them. She briefly closed her eyes but did not utter a word.

"Can we sit down?" asked Hunter. "This isn't something to be discussed in a hallway."

"Yes, of course," said William, turning to his right. He ushered us into a formal room made cozier by several pieces of large furniture. Three oversized couches and two armchairs were in the center of the room and a piano in the back. "Please take a seat."

Hunter and I took the couch while William and Anne sat directly in front of us. Anne sat back and crossed her legs. William, however, sat perched at the edge of the couch with his elbows on his knees, eager to learn what had happened. I gulped.

"We did indeed find your father," began Hunter. "Well, actually, he found me first. Or I should say, he was the one who kidnapped me."

"What are you talking about?" said William. "I was there at the church. That man was not my father."

"No, but he worked for him," explained Hunter.

William's knee, the one that was bouncing earlier, now stopped. "Worked for him? Are you sure?"

"Yes," said Hunter, and paused when William shook his head.

"You must be mistaken. Why would my father do that?" asked William.

Hunter pursed his lips and leaned forward, elbows on his knees now, too. "Your father wanted to lure Michaela into the caves."

"Why?" asked William, still shaking his head.

"Because he believed sacrificing her would bring your brother Erik back."

Glancing at me, then back to Hunter, he said, "Why would he believe that?"

"Hel appeared to him in a dream. He believed sacrificing the blood of the woman who'd killed Erik would return him home."

When William's head bounced between us, Hunter added, "Michaela's mother killed Erik."

Anne gasped but covered the sound with her hand. However, William's sharp intake of breath had already overpowered it. "What did you say?" he asked, his eyes widening.

"Erik had completely lost control and had killed several humans. Michaela's mother hunted him down and killed him."

"How?" pleaded William.

"We don't know the details," explained Hunter.

"Then how did my father learn that it was Michaela's mother that had killed Erik?"

Hunter ran his fingers through his dark hair. "Because my aunt Elenora told him. She knew about Michaela's mother, and when we kicked her out of the kingdom, she decided to ruffle some feathers."

William turned his amber eyes on me. Instead of the anger I had expected, they glistened in anguish. "Your mother killed him?"

Tears welled up in my own eyes, empathizing with the pain in William's voice. "Yes," I whispered.

William dropped his head in his hands and rubbed his forehead. "But why come after Michaela?"

"Michaela's mom is dead. Michaela's blood would be the closest one for the sacrifice."

William's head shook in his hands. Then the muffled words came out, "My God. I am so sorry."

Relief at hearing those words caught me off guard, and a small sob escaped my mouth. I covered it, but my body shook. William still had not heard the whole story, and his next words confirmed it.

"Where is he? Are you taking him back with you to New York?" he asked.

When Hunter said nothing, William lifted his head.

"He's dead," said Hunter. William's stricken face tore at my heart. Tears streamed down my face. But Hunter wasn't finished. "I killed him," he said, looking directly at William. His chest heaved and his jaw sawed back and forth. "I'm sorry, William. But he gave me no choice. I couldn't risk him coming for my family."

Anne reached over and wrapped herself onto her husband's back. William's body shook, a sob wailed from his mouth, and I had to look away. Hunter reached for my hand, but I couldn't turn around to face him. As much as I knew all the terrible crimes Hans had committed, I still hated what we had done.

"How did you both escape?" asked Anne, looking up from her husband's shoulder.

"We fought," said Hunter.

"Alexander helped me," I added.

"Alexander Larsen?" asked William, his head snapping up.

I nodded, and William shook his head. "I feel like everything I knew to be right was all wrong. My father was a good man, a philanthropist."

"Your mother set up the charities after your brother disappeared," said Anne softly. "She attended the events and raised the money. I don't think your father ever cared about it."

William looked back at his wife, his eyes searching hers, then dropped his head again.

"He never got over his grief," said William, his voice muffled in his hands.

A fresh tear fell down my face. My heart broke for William. I searched for a tissue and when I didn't find one; I excused myself to use the bathroom. Hunter let go of my hand but watched me as I crossed the room. *I'm okay*, I mouthed to him, and he nodded.

The soles of my flat shoes tapped across the porcelain hallway and the sound was deafening in the empty house. Perhaps my nerves were just on edge right now.

The powder room was quite large. It had a cushioned stool that I sat on for a minute while I gathered myself back together. I knew it was triggering for me to be there when William heard his father was killed since I'd lost mine at such a young age. Watching William's face, I realized it hurt to lose a parent at any age and any circumstance.

After taking a few fortifying breaths, I felt strong enough to go back to the room. But when I stepped out of the bathroom, I ran into Mathias.

"Oof," I said, and steadied myself, placing both hands on Mathias's chest. "We really need to stop bumping into each other like this." Then my heart sank.

Mathias didn't know what had happened to his father, and we'd have to tell the story all over again. "Mathias, come with me to the living room. There's something you should know."

I tried to pull my hands away, but Mathias caught them tightly in his grip. I looked down at his hands and his knuckles were white.

"Mathias, you're hurting me," I said and tried again to pull away, but he clenched tighter. Pain shot through my wrist and up my arm. I looked at Mathias and his amber eyes blazed like a stoked fire and his lips were a razor-sharp line slashed across his face.

"Come with me," he growled and pulled me into another room. He slammed the door shut with his foot and pushed me up against the wall. My head slammed hard against it. I closed my eyes for just a moment until the pain subsided.

"I know what happened," he snarled. His face, only inches from mine, flushed with anger. "How did you do it?" he whispered harshly.

I shook my head because I refused to speak to him while he held me down like this.

"How did you do it!" he roared this time.

My legs shook, and my heart raced. I knew Mathias was angry, and I just wanted him to calm down before he lost control of his instincts and hurt me.

"Mathias, I will tell you everything that happened, but you have to let me go first," I said slowly and enunciated each word.

He shook his head. "No," he spat. "I don't trust you. Your mother killed my brother and now you killed my father. You will tell me what happened."

Mathias squeezed my wrists tighter with each word, and I feared my bones would snap.

"All right," I said. "My mother killed your brother, but I didn't kill your father."

He pushed his body against mine and I could barely breathe from the weight of him against me. "Liar," he sneered.

"I'm not lying," I whispered, barely able to speak. "Hunter killed him."

Mathias stared at me, and I kept my gaze steady. "If that is true, he did it because of you."

I couldn't deny the truth of that statement, but I could explain. "Your father intended to hurt him—kill him even—before he killed me. Hunter would not let that happen."

Mathias must have realized the truth behind my words because his grip loosened, but only a fraction. It was enough to give me hope.

"He had a team of manticores there, including *The Mammoth*. How did you escape?" he asked.

This time, it was me that stared at him. "We never mentioned anything about *The Mammoth* to William. How do you know he was there?"

Mathias's eye twitched. "Answer me!" he shouted.

"Not until you answer me," I ground out. He just stared, and I didn't back down. "You knew, didn't you? You knew what your father was up to."

Mathias sneered. "He told me about his dream. I was the one who came up with the plan to draw you to Norway. Two brutal murders would grab the attention of the king and he'd send his son. I'd heard

Hunter was madly in love and knew he'd never leave his wife behind."

"You killed two innocent people?"

"They were not innocent," he bit out. "The police chief was incompetent, and that woman helped your mother."

What was he talking about? He was insane.

"Let me go and we'll discuss this. I know you're angry, Mathias. But hurting me will change nothing."

Mathias's face hardened once more. "I disagree. Ever since you discovered manticores, you've left a trail of dead bodies behind you." He brought his lips down to my ear. "There is something about you. A temptress. I can feel it in my body." He pushed his body up against me and I felt his arousal. My mind spun. This could not be happening.

"Get off of me, you asshole," I hissed, but he just pushed himself harder against me. I closed my eyes. As scared as I was, I didn't want to stop his heart. I didn't want to leave, as he said, another dead body behind me. Although I could only be blamed for John's death, his words affected me and I wondered if my presence caused the demise of the others.

"Yes," he hissed. "This is a much better idea than the other one."

I struggled against his hold but he didn't budge.

"I was going to wrap my hands around this pretty little neck until it snapped, but now I think a more pleasurable idea has presented itself. Why not make this worth my while." He ground his hips against me and bile burned its way up my throat. "Both would kill you, but this way has piqued my interest."

I stomped my foot on top of his shoe.

"Ow!" he shouted but did not loosen his grip on my wrists.

Pulling my knee up, I hit him hard in the groin. He let go of me then, dropping his hands to clutch himself. I opened the door, but he slammed it shut again and threw me down to the floor. In a flash, his body was on top of mine.

I pushed against his shoulders, his chest, shouting, "Get off of me!" but he was a manticore and much stronger than me.

His hand snaked up my skirt and pulled down my panties. My breath came out in a whoosh and I closed my eyes. No way would I let this monster rape me.

No fucking way.

I began a chant that would put him to sleep, but halfway through, he unzipped his pants and positioned himself on top of me. For a second, I imagined him doing this to someone else. If he could murder two people in cold blood and do such a thing to me, what would stop him from hurting someone else?

I could stop him.

In that instance, I made my decision. I recalled a chant I hadn't used before but had read in my mother's books. The words rushed out of my mouth in a single breath.

Mathias let out a piercing scream, his body taut on top of mine, right before he shriveled onto the ground next to me. This time, I heard the bones break in his body, each one, one by one, and I stood there and watched. I raised my fist in the air, his wide eyes pinned to my hands, following my movement.

"You're right," I said. "There is something special about me and now you know it."

His eyes no longer blazed but watered instead. I could only imagine the excoriating pain he must feel. I didn't care one bit. "I won't let you hurt anyone else, you monster."

I curled my fists and imagined his beating heart in the palm of my hand. I squeezed, feeling each pump pulsating against my fingers. Mathias arched his back. I pressed harder until his eyes rolled behind his head and his body went limp. I slammed my fist down on my thigh and panted next to him. He didn't move.

I killed him.

I spun and grabbed the potted plant next to me and vomited into the base. My body convulsed and heaved as I continued to retch until nothing came out. I fell to my knees and sobbed. This was no accident like John's death. I'd intentionally killed Mathias. Realizing that I'd do it all over again, I clutched my chest as another sob racked through my body. I knew, without a doubt, I'd lost another piece of my soul. I bit hard onto my lip and let the tears stream down my face. Slowly, I slid down onto the floor and curled myself into a ball next to Mathias's still body.

Twenty-Five

Hunter

Michaela had been in the bathroom for quite some time. William had recovered from the shocking news. At least he could now ask about details without squeezing the couch cushions beside him. He even apologized when I told him how they tortured me for hours.

I checked my watch for the third time. It had been at least twenty minutes since Michaela had left the room.

I should go check on her.

"Excuse me a moment," I said to William and Anne and walked out into the hallway. It was empty and when I rounded the corner, the door to the powder room was open. I stepped toward it and when I got closer, realized it was empty. I strode to the opposite end of the hallway from which I'd come. As I walked past a closed door, my chest tightened. A strange feeling came over me. Turning back to the door, I knocked. When there was no answer, I turned the handle and opened it a sliver, but it was enough to take in the scene before me. It took a minute for my mind to process what my eyes drank in. *Michaela—laying on the floor—*in the fetal position.

I ran into the room and dropped to my knees beside her. I pulled her hair away from her face and felt the dampness on my fingers. Her whole cheek was wet.

"Michaela," I said, hearing the panic in my voice. "Michaela, are you all right, sweetheart?"

She shook her head and squeezed her eyes shut tighter still. A sob wailed from her lips, then she cried in earnest. I pulled her up and held her head against my chest. Her whole body shook, and I ran my hands up and down her arms. "Are you hurt?"

She shook her head again and continued to cry. That was when I saw him. I don't know how I missed him when I came into the room, except I panicked when I saw her on the ground and saw nothing else in my periphery. But now that I held her in my arms, I assessed Mathias laying on the ground next to her, his lips slightly blue and his face deathly pale.

I pressed her tighter against me. "What happened?" I whispered, then spotted something else on the ground. I couldn't make out the black fabric at first but soon recognized the lace from her undergarments. Then I knew.

"Mathias..." she began, her body shaking in my arms.

"Shh—" I said, the realization choking me. She didn't need to say anything more or explain herself. My heart knew hers well enough to understand what had happened here.

"Shh. You did the right thing," I told her.

"Hunter—" she wept. "I killed him..." Her voice broke and so did my heart at hearing her pain.

"I wish I could have done it," I said. "I hope you weren't merciful." I wanted him to still be alive only so I could rip him apart myself, limb from limb, starting with the one between his legs.

"I was ruthless," she said, looking up at me and didn't stutter. "I could have put him to sleep, but I wanted him dead. I didn't want him to hurt anyone else."

I pressed her head back against my chest and I stared up at the ceiling. "My God, Michaela. You humble me."

Even when taking a life, she did it not only for herself but for others. I am not worthy of her love. I would have taken pleasure from ending his life, the hell with everyone else. No one would have crossed my mind. I held her in my arms for countless minutes, giving her all the time she needed to recover. If not fully, at least enough time to stand up and leave the room.

"What do we do now?" she asked.

I ran my fingers through her hair and pulled her back, staring into her eyes. "Do you feel strong enough to tell William and Anne what happened here? I would understand if you don't want to."

She looked away for a minute. I imagined contemplating the words she would say, then she nodded. "Yes, I'll tell them. They need to know the whole truth."

"Well, I'm not sure about the whole truth," I reminded her. "We can't exactly tell them what you did."

"Why not, Hunter?" she asked. "We have to start trusting manticores outside of the kingdom too. We should start with our friends."

"You consider William and Anne our friends?" I wondered what I had missed while trapped in that cave.

"Yes. Anne helped me find you and she kept your whereabouts from her husband. She put you first in that case. I feel we can trust them with this."

"All right. But let's keep it simple." I thought about the exact words to say and came up empty. She must have noticed my struggle.

"We tell them I have special gifts. That I can control a manticore's heart."

I wasn't too sure about this. The professor had always warned me to tell no one the specifics of what Michaela was. But even he had rescinded a bit by allowing Michaela to teach at the academy. She taught our young manticores what Sheds are and that they are not the natural enemies of manticores. Perhaps we can try to test this outside of the academy, with, as Michaela called them, our friends.

"All right. Let's go with the truth. Secrets just come so naturally to me."

"Yes, we need to work on that," she said. She did not smile, but the words gave me hope that she would be all right.

I pulled Michaela up next to me. "Let's go speak to William and Anne." She nodded and led the way.

When we returned to the living room, William was pouring himself a drink and Anne sat with her legs crossed on the couch. Her eyes immediately went to Michaela's, and she stood from the couch. "Michaela, is everything all right?" she asked, her eyes roaming across Michaela's body.

Michaela shook her head but kept her composure. "No, Anne. It's not," she said.

"You'd better sit down, William," continued Michaela. I did not sit, worried that William could not handle the news of his brother's death on top of losing his father today. It was a lot to ask of a man, especially a protective manticore.

"I ran into Mathias when I stepped out of the powder room," she began. "He seemed upset, and I tried to calm him down."

William put his drink down on the side table, and Anne placed her hand on his knee.

"He pulled me into another room and slammed the door closed." Michaela's voice hitched at this last part, and I sat down next to her and held her hand. She nodded and continued. "He tried to rape me," she whispered.

"What!" roared William. "The bastard. How could he do something like that? Michaela, I am so sorry." He stood. "I will speak to him and nothing like this will ever happen again."

When Michaela kept her head down and I continued to stare at her hand, Anne must have realized there was more. She grabbed her husband's hand and pulled him back down onto the couch. "I think Michaela took care of it herself already," she said. Michaela nodded, and tears formed in her eyes again.

"What happened?" asked Anne.

"I killed him," whispered Michaela.

"You *killed* him?" repeated William. "What do you mean, you *killed* him?"

"He's dead, William," I said. "But I'm not sorry about it. I wish I could have stopped him before he attacked my wife."

At the mention of the word 'wife', William flinched, then looked toward his own spouse. "Where is he now?"

"He's in the library." I stood to accompany William. "Michaela, why don't you and Anne wait here."

She nodded and Anne moved to take my place on the couch next to Michaela. Before I quit the room with William, Anne had her arm around Michaela's shoulder. I sighed a breath of relief that Michaela was right. She had found a friend in Anne. I hoped she was right about William, too.

William led the way down the narrow hall and nearly raced to the library. However, he stopped abruptly as soon as he entered the room. "*Mathias*," he whispered and covered his mouth with his hand. "Oh Mathias, what have you done this time?" He crouched down beside his brother and cupped the side of his face. "He had not always done the right thing, but he was my brother."

William's throat worked furiously, but no words came out of his mouth. He ran his hand over his face again and paced the room. "I just can't believe it," he said finally. "I went to bed last night with my entire family intact and now I'm an orphan with no family." He cleared his throat, fighting back his emotion.

"You have family, William. You have Anne and your sons. And you have friends, too. You have me and Michaela. We won't abandon you. You have welcomed us into your home and Anne helped Michaela when she needed her. That will not go unnoticed. You are welcome to return to New York with us if you wish. We can find a place for you within our kingdom."

"You'd be willing to do that, after everything my family has done to you?"

I tilted my head. "I know better than anyone else that we cannot judge a person based on their kinship." I smiled with no real amusement. "I've learned to judge people on their own actions and your actions have been honorable."

A sob escaped through William's throat, and he bit his fist to hold it in. "Thank you, Hunter, but our place is here. I will rebuild what my father and brother destroyed and make the Pedersen name proud again."

I walked over to William and placed my hand on his shoulder. "I have no doubt you will, my friend."

William nodded, but then pivoted swiftly, my arm falling by my side.

"Wait! Did you see that?" William crouched down next to his brother.

"See what?" I asked.

"He moved his lips."

I felt bad for William, seeing things that weren't there, fighting for hope. "William—" I began, but then noticed Mathias's face no longer held the same deathly pallor as before.

"I hear a faint heartbeat," he said, his ear to Mathias's chest.

Then the bastard opened his eyes.

"Mathias," William cried, pulling his brother's face toward him. "Can you hear me?"

Mathias's eyes bounced around the room, unable to focus on anything until they reached mine. He locked in with my gaze and anger boiled in the pit of my stomach, rising through my chest, and spewing out of my throat in a loud, guttural roar. "I'm going to fucking kill you!"

I lunged for him, but William stopped me. He held me back, latching himself onto my back and pulling me away from his brother.

"What's going on?" Anne said from the doorway.

Michaela followed right behind her. "Oh my God," she whispered and fell forward, clutching the doorknob.

I threw William off of me and ran to hold her up.

"He's alive?" she asked, her eyes roaming over Mathias's body. He was still prone on the floor, but his eyes zeroed in on her.

"Not for long," I growled. She pulled me back when I walked away.

William put his hands on my chest. "I know you are angry," he said. "But let's discuss this."

"There's nothing to discuss, William."

"Yes, there is. He will be punished, but I will take him to New York. Let the king decide. I will abide by the ruling, I promise."

"Yes, but will he," I said, pointing to the predator on the floor.

"I will take it upon myself to ensure that he does," he said. Then, moving both hands to Hunter's shoulders, he begged. "Please, Hunter."

That one word, *please,* did me in. The pain behind it poured cool water over my anger.

"We leave tomorrow," I said. "Be on that plane with him."

"Tomorrow," William agreed.

"Make it a separate flight," whispered Michaela. "I don't want to be anywhere near him."

"I understand," said William.

Anne put her arm over Michaela, their heads close together, and walked her out of the room.

***

Michaela tossed and turned as she slept in our bed. When she whimpered, I brought my lips close to her ear and tried to soothe her. "Shh, you're all right. You're safe. No one will hurt you."

I lay next to her but didn't touch her. I wasn't sure if she wanted a man's touch at that moment. My words worked and her body relaxed, falling back asleep. Only to start again a little while later.

When she opened her eyes the next morning, red and raw, I couldn't hold back. I drew her into my arms and buried my face in her hair.

She held me and wept, each tear burning my flesh.

"I wanted him dead. I wish he were dead," she cried.

"Then I'll take care of it," I vowed.

"No. You don't understand." She shook her head. "I wanted to kill him. I wanted to punish him for what he had done."

"You did."

She pushed her hair back from her face. "Yes, but somehow the bastard survived."

I held her tighter, unsure of what else to say.

"He will pay for what he did to you, I swear." The sweet taste of my venom flooded my mouth. I closed my eyes to calm my instincts down.

Pulling away from my arms, she rose from the bed and wiped her tears away. "It's over, Hunter. The king will deal with him. I just want to go home and get back to Violet."

She walked to the bathroom and closed the door behind her. I fell back onto the pillows, swinging my arm over my eyes.

Twenty-Six

Hunter

Astrid waited for us in the lobby as we checked out of the hotel. She wore her brown leather pants and clutched her brown felt hat as she approached us.

"I'll be right back," I said to Michaela and met Astrid halfway.

"I had my suspicions about the Pedersens, but I honestly didn't think they were capable of such violence," she said when I reached her.

I nodded and looked past her to the busy street outside. "I don't think Hans was in his right mind. He was only thinking of getting his son back." Turning my gaze back to Astrid, I said in a low voice. "You know how it is once we lose control of our anger. Our instincts overpower reason and we become monsters."

I hated the truth in my words. What I'd done to Hans and wanted to do to Mathias wasn't any better than what Hans had done to me. I told myself that Mathias's victims were innocent, while he was not. It eased my conscience somewhat.

Astrid tilted her head, watching me, and I turned away.

When I stepped outside, Astrid lit a cigarette and offered one to me. I declined and watched Michaela as she finished checking out and walked toward us.

"She seems tough, your wife," continued Astrid. "Yet I still don't understand how the two of you fought an army of manticores besides her saying some chants," she sucked in a drag of her cigarette. "But I've seen stranger things in my lifetime."

"I'm sure you have," I smiled.

She blew out the smoke and both our eyes landed on a red sports car pulling up at the side of the road. "Well, if it isn't the manticore godfather," she sneered. Then dropped her cigarette on the ground and put it out with her boot.

Michaela walked up to us at that moment and interlaced her fingers with mine. "Is that Alexander?" she asked, shielding her eyes from the sun.

"It is," I said.

Michaela had filled me in on her conversation with Alexander. I forgave him for not telling me about his uncle's involvement because he had saved Michaela's life. But I didn't trust the manticore. He was cunning and not afraid to throw his family to the lions if it meant he would gain greater control and expand his wealth. I narrowed my eyes as he pulled his car up to the curb. "I wonder what he's doing here," I said.

"About that," Michaela replied. He's coming back to New York with us."

"He is?" I asked. "Why?"

"I told you in the car ride back from the mountains, but you were too exhausted to remember. I think it's best if we keep Alexander close to us. He's going to be on the King's Council, so we need to get to know him better. Understand what he's about."

"I know what he's about. I've seen manticores like him before. They're destructive and don't care who they hurt to get what they want. But I'll tolerate him for the plane ride back to New York."

"One more thing," she said and squeezed my hand tighter. "He's also asked for another reward for helping me save you," she continued.

"What kind of reward does he want?" I stared at the bulk of the manticore sitting in the flashy car in front of us, wearing a black suit and aviator glasses.

She shook her head. "I have no idea," she whispered.

Why did that sound ominous?

***

The next morning, the five of us boarded a plane headed to New York City—me, Michaela, Alexander, Vivienne, and Nicholas. I ensured William and Mathias got on the flight before us. Thomas would meet them at the airport and take them back to the kingdom. Sitting next to Michaela on the plane, she worked on her laptop while my attention zeroed in on Alexander. I knew little about the manticore, other than he ran nightclubs in Norway and was one of the richest men in the country. I knew he was building a reputation for himself and with Hans, Mathias, and his uncle out of the way, we may have just cleared a path for him to the top. He was sharp. I'd give him that. He was also ambitious and ruthless. While I did not regret his actions against my aunt Elenora, it made me wonder what else he was capable of.

I dropped my head back against the airplane pillow and considered the events in Norway and how I would explain everything to my father. Astrid was relieved we had found the killer and would bring him before the king in New York. She was even okay with Hans's demise. "I do not appreciate vigilante justice," she had said. "But he had it coming."

Astrid had sent a cleanup crew to the cave. She had ensured Hans Pedersen's death was attributed to a car accident. The mayor was a different story. Video evidence pointed to his involvement in those ghastly murders. But they found him dead, hanging in a cave, with a suicide note next to him detailing his remorse. With no other evidence, the police closed the case.

Michaela swiveled her laptop toward me. "I want to show you

something," she said. I leaned forward, looking at some woman's social media page. "What am I looking at?" I asked.

"That's Evelyn Berg," she said with a smile.

"Is that name supposed to mean something to me?"

"Not really. Something Mathias said bothered me. He mentioned the woman had it coming because she had helped my mother. When I looked into his last victim, I didn't see the connection at first. What does a woman who likes to bake and garden have to do with Erik or my mother? Then I noticed in one of her pictures she wore a uniform. When I zoomed in on the logo, I recognized the Norwegian airline. I asked Olivia to look into the airline's employee records in 2007 to see if she could find her and bam, there she was."

"So she worked for an airline in 2007. What does that have to do with your mother?"

She grinned as though she had discovered the world's greatest secret, and in our little world, she possibly had. "My mother boarded a flight in 2007. She had told Nicholas she almost didn't get on that flight because police were looking for a woman that fit her description." Her finger moved from her chin to tap on her bottom lip. "Probably your father's men."

She waved that off and sat up straighter. "Anyway, she said the woman had told the police that without a warrant, they could not stop the flight. My mother must have lost them at the airport when she landed in Montreal. According to Nicholas, she never took a direct flight home in case they ever followed her."

"Smart woman, your mother," I said, processing the information.

"They fired Evelyn from her job about a week ago. A report in her employee file Olivia had found showed the complaint had come from none other than Mathias Pedersen. Of course, someone as powerful as Pedersen could get an employee fired with a simple phone call. But why would he want to do that? Unless it was personal. We now know why. If I'd just found this sooner, maybe we could have stopped Hans before he took you and Nicholas."

I smiled when I saw the tenacity in her eyes. Like a lioness who had cornered her prey. "You're pretty smart for putting that all together."

After putting away her laptop, she grinned at me with a Cheshire cat smile. She interlaced her hands across her middle. "I would have figured it out and caught Hans, you know." She then put her index finger and thumb together. "I was this close. Once I made the connection with Mathias, we would have stopped him and his father. I just needed one more day."

I chuckled at her confidence. "I always wondered how your mother got to the rogue manticores before my father's men. Now, I know why." I leaned down and kissed her smiling lips. "My father's manticores tracked with their noses and not their minds."

Her lips spread into a sweet smile and opened softly for me. I slid my tongue across her top lip and pulled it in gently with my teeth. A growl escaped from my lips and while no human had noticed, the two other manticores, all turned in my direction. I laughed and pulled her close to my chest. She wrapped her arms around me and we stayed that way until the sun rose in the clouds the next morning over JFK airport.

"Where will you be staying in New York?" Michaela asked Alexander after we'd retrieved our luggage from the carousel.

"Can the kingdom accommodate me while I'm in town?" he asked.

"There are a few beds there, but it's not exactly The Ritz," I explained.

"You can stay with me," said Vivienne. She didn't smile, but I knew her well enough to know when she was interested in someone. I felt no jealousy, of course, relief perhaps. We had both finally moved on.

"Hunter, I'd like to give the king my version of the events," said Nicholas, walking behind us toward the exit.

"I'm not sure if that's necessary, but I will speak to my father. The trial should be sometime tomorrow afternoon," I said over my shoulder.

"I'll call you tomorrow, Nicholas, and let you know," said Michaela as we walked through the automated glass doors. Several cars lined the pickup lane and swarms of people stood in a long queue for a taxi. Thankfully, I'd arranged for Tony to pick us up.

"Dad!" a familiar voice called from the street.

"Adam?" Michaela asked beside me. Indeed, Nicholas's son, and Michaela's *friend*, was running toward us. I knew she didn't have feelings for him, but I disliked him, nonetheless.

"What's Adam doing here?" asked Michaela. "Wasn't he in Italy?"

"Yes, he was," said Nicholas.

But when Adam approached, it was clear he wasn't happy to see his father, but angry. *Ah, he knows.* "Someone told him about Nicholas' kidnapping," I said.

"I didn't say a word," exclaimed Michaela.

"I may have mentioned something," Nicholas said, his hands up in the air. "When he couldn't get a hold of me, I had to tell him why."

"Oh Nicholas," Michaela sighed. "This isn't good."

Adam finally reached us and immediately went to embrace his father. "Are you all right?" he asked while patting the older man's shoulder and visually examining him from head to toe.

"I'm fine. I'm fine," said Nicholas. "Stop your fussing."

"Fussing?" cried Adam. "You were kidnapped—in a foreign country—by a manticore!"

"I needed a little adventure in my life," Nicholas chuckled.

"This isn't funny, Dad," he said. "They could have killed you."

Michaela's face fell with the reminder.

I led her toward the black SUV that had just pulled up in front of us. Tony was already out and opening the door for Michaela.

"Where are you going?" asked Adam. "I'm not done asking questions."

I sighed but knew Adam had a right to know what had happened with his father. "Meet us at our place."

"Fine," said Adam. "Take my dad with you. I'm parked in the next lot and I don't want to over-tire him, especially after everything he's been through."

I shook my head. "He really hasn't complained about it—" but at Adam's hard stare I raised my hands, realizing once again, now wasn't the time to argue with Adam about semantics. "We'll see you there."

Adam nodded once and walked back toward his car. I climbed into the passenger seat of the SUV and looked back. Nicholas sat in the next row with Michaela while Vivienne and Alexander cozied up in the back.

"Thanks, Tony," I said, turning back to the front. "We better go. I have a feeling Adam will be outside waiting for us."

***

I was right. Adam stood with his arms crossed in front of our building by the time Tony pulled up. "Tony will take you back to your place," I said to Vivienne, stepping out of the car.

"Thank you," she said with a nod.

Michaela stepped out, turning her head toward Vivienne and Alexander. "I'll see you later."

I unloaded our bags and the four of us—Adam, Nicholas, Michaela, and I headed inside.

When we reached our floor, I stepped off the elevator and opened the door to our penthouse.

"Michaela, you're back!" cried Ramona. A huge grin spread across my face as I watched my wife approach her grandmother, holding Violet in her arms.

"Dadadada," Violet babbled. "No, mama. I'm mama," said Michaela, extending her hands to pick up our girl. She nuzzled her neck and planted kiss after kiss on her cheeks. "Oh, I missed you so much."

"How's daddy's little girl?" I asked, coming up behind Michaela, resting my hand on her shoulder.

"Dadadada," Violet shouted, her hands flapping in the air. I chuckled and kissed the top of her head. "God, it feels good to be home." I gathered them both in my arms, rubbing Michaela's back.

"Thank you for taking care of her, Ramona," I said.

"It was my pleasure." She removed her apron after washing her hands. "Nicholas, it is wonderful to see you again." She came up to him and greeted him with a kiss on each cheek.

"And you, Ramona," said Nicholas. He motioned toward his son. "You remember Adam."

"Nice to see you again, Adam," my grandmother replied and patted his cheek.

"Likewise," Adam said, but his stern face argued otherwise.

"Why doesn't everyone get comfortable? I'll prepare us a drink," said Hunter.

"Make Adam's a double," my grandmother whispered to me. I bit back a laugh, but Violet giggled in my arms.

"*Piccolina* understood me. Ah, she's so smart," said my grandmother, pinching Violet's cheek. Violet thought it was the funniest thing she'd ever heard and let out a peal of laughter.

Adam, on the other hand, wasn't laughing at all. Instead, he stood in front of Nicholas, who sat down on the couch with his arms crossed. "So, who's going to tell me what the hell happened in Norway?"

Twenty-Seven

Michaela

Manticores sat shoulder to shoulder in the courtroom, several had to stand in the back. Everyone came to see the killer. Or perhaps they came to see the one who had his heart stopped momentarily and lived to tell the story. Either way, Hunter said it hadn't been this crowded since they'd caught Jenkins. I sat in the front row with Hunter and Nicholas by my side. William and Adam sat on the bench with us, while Alexander and Vivienne were several pews behind.

"Everyone rise for King Marsel Durand," called Lord Chancellor Lee, wearing a formal military uniform with medals streaming down the front pockets. I wondered how many armies he had led in his lifetime.

The king walked into the courtroom, his back straight, his head held high. He was a sweet and considerate father-in-law, but in the courtroom, his austere face made me shiver. "Please, be seated," he said as he sat down on his brass throne.

"Mathias Pedersen, come stand before me," called the king.

Mathias stood and approached the throne. Two guards flanked either side of him. His eyes were bloodshot and his pale skin had not fully recovered. *Good.*

"You stand before me, charged with the murder of Jan Olsen and Evelyn Berg. How do you plead?"

"Not guilty," he said.

A murmur rose among the crowd. The king leaned forward. "Do you deny killing those people?"

"I do not, but it was not murder, it was revenge. They helped the actual killer get away." He shifted his eyes to me and pointed. "Her mother."

The crowd grew louder.

"Order," shouted Lord Chancellor Lee, and the room quieted down.

"Lucia Shedly is not on trial here today," said the king. "Your defense is semantics, at best." Then he skewered Mathias with a stare. "You are a coward for killing those humans in cold blood. Do you have no other words to explain yourself before I sentence you?"

"My king," said William, rising from his seat. "I'm here to beg for my brother's life. I know what he did was inexcusable but I ask that you do not execute him." Then, dropping his voice, he begged. "Please."

The king watched William, closed his eyes briefly, then turned to Hunter. He gave a slight nod, probably imperceptible to anyone else, but I noticed. "I will consider it."

"Do you have anything else to add?" the king asked Mathias.

His lips twisted in an ugly smile. "Will you not ask me about the other incident?"

My stomach dropped. I'd asked the king not to mention what happened in the library at trial. It was enough Mathias was up against two murder charges. I didn't want the details of what happened between us aired out in the courtroom. I would rather not live through it again. But at Mathias's words, my heart raced, and I squeezed Hunter's arm.

He stood, but the king raised his hand.

"I know what you did, Mathias. I do not need nor want to hear any defense for that."

Mathias frowned but kept his mouth shut.

"In light of William's plea, and all that he's done for Michaela and Hunter, I will spare you your life," said the king. "But you will live the rest of your days in the dungeons below. However, many years you have left, you'll spend them regretting your actions." Turning to the guard, he added, "Take him downstairs, now."

William dropped his head in his hands, and his shoulders shook. I rubbed his back but could not bring myself to speak any words to comfort him. I was glad his brother could hurt no one else.

Hunter held my hand and I let the emotions of the last two days wash through me. I would never be clean of the memories but felt some of the grit fall off of me. I buried my face into Hunter's chest and he ran his fingers through my hair. When his hand stilled, I sat up straight in the pew. Hunter watched someone approach.

"Alexander," he said.

"I was hoping we could speak to the king now about my reward and favor," said Alexander. He certainly did not wish to waste any time.

Hunter stood. "Come with me, and I'll see if he's ready to receive you." He reached down and extended his hand to me. I grasped it and the three of us walked out of the courtroom together toward the king's chambers.

The chamber was located just outside of the courtroom, the room just a few steps from where we exited. Hunter knocked on the wooden door and the sound echoed throughout the hallway.

"Enter," said the king, and Hunter opened the door for me and Alexander.

"Father, this is Alexander Larsen. He is the one I had told you about. His information led Michaela to find Hans Pedersen and me. We offered a place on your council to anyone with information leading to the rogue manticore's capture."

"Yes, I recall the agreement. Please sit." He extended his hand toward the two chairs in front of him.

"Go ahead," said Hunter to Alexander and me.

"I'd rather stand," said Alexander.

Hunter looked pointedly at him. "It would be rude to do so when your king has asked you to sit."

Without another word, Alexander took the seat next to me.

"Good. Now, I should explain how the council works and the role you will play," began the king. "We meet monthly in my chambers to discuss kingdom events. I will seek your counsel but ultimately make the final decision."

Alexander nodded.

"I may ask you to fulfill a mission on behalf of the kingdom, but those assignments are quite rare. However, I need to know that you are prepared to do my bidding."

"I am," said Alexander.

"Good. The first meeting is next week. You might as well stay until then. Do you plan to move permanently to New York City?

"No. I do not, sire."

The king frowned. "Do you plan to fly back here each month?"

"Yes."

"Well, suit yourself," said the king, and looked down at some papers on his desk. "That is all," he said in dismissal.

"There's one more thing, sire," said Alexander. The king looked up. "I made another arrangement with Michaela back in Norway. She agreed to grant me another favor. The king pointed his gaze at me and I squirmed a bit in my seat."

"I haven't had a chance to mention this to you yet," I explained. While my father-in-law may have laughed it off, the king before me remained unmoved. He focused his attention back on Alexander and I let out a breath I didn't realize I was holding.

"What is the favor you seek?"

"I want to take Michaela back with me to Norway."

Everyone in the room shouted at once.

"*What?*"

"*Are you insane?*"

"*Excuse me?*"

I stood up and looked down at Alexander. "I am not a commodity to be traded in for a favor. Choose something else." I kept my voice steady, despite hearing the growl from Hunter behind me.

Alexander raised his arms in defeat. "Fine. I thought you wouldn't agree to that, so I came prepared with something else."

The king nodded, and Alexander continued. "I want to be appointed magistrate in Norway. I want Astrid's position."

Stunned, I sat back down in my seat. Having denied him his first request, it would seem unfair to do the same with his second. *Perhaps that was his plan from the start.*

"Father?" asked Hunter, his voice soft.

The king raised his hand. "I cannot do this. Astrid has been a loyal magistrate," then moving his eyes to stare at Alexander he added, "I trust her implicitly."

"I understand," said Alexander and leaned forward toward the king's desk. "But how would it look if I told other manticores that the king not only refused my favor but refused my amended offer? It would seem unreasonable, no?"

Yes, Alexander was a cunning creature.

The king knew it, too. He leaned back in his chair and crossed his arms. "Fine," he said.

A smile spread across Alexander's face and he leaned back in his chair as well, resting his clasped hands on his lean abdomen.

I wanted to wipe that smirk right off his face but knew our hands were tied. I had promised him a favor and knew he was capable of asking for one this big. He could have asked for money, lots of it, but for someone like Alexander, power was priceless.

"You are dismissed," said the king with a growl. We rose from our seats, Alexander with a bit more bounce in his step, and left the king's chambers.

"Alexander," Hunter called out as the manticore walked away from us in the hallway. He turned to face Hunter, hands in his pockets and a smile playing on his lips.

"Yes?"

"I would watch your back if I were you," he said. "You've just put a big target on it. I don't think Astrid will take this lightly."

"I'll be ready," he said, his face unchanged.

Hunter placed his hand at the small of my back, and we walked away.

"Oh, and Michaela?" he called.

I turned to face him again. He took a step closer to me. "I've heard some pretty interesting rumors about you since I arrived in New York."

My heartbeat faltered, but I kept my face serene.

"Don't worry, your secret is safe with me," he said with a wink and strode off.

"Why must everything be so complicated?" I huffed after Alexander was out of earshot.

Hunter put his arm around me as we walked down the oak floored hallway, deep underneath Central Park. "Because life as a manticore and a manticore's wife is never dull. I can promise you that."

"That's what I'm afraid of," I sighed, but leaned into Hunter's embrace.

Twenty-Eight

Hunter

After dealing with the trial and the unexpected demands from Alexander, Michaela said she was ready to go home. I wasn't quite finished yet.

"Will you be all right to go back with Adam and Nicholas?" I asked.

"Yes. Of course," she said. "You're sure you can't take care of whatever it is tomorrow?"

"I'm sure. I need to speak with the professor about something and might as well do it now since I'm already here at the kingdom."

"I understand." She stood on her tiptoes to kiss me and I sipped her lips like my favorite whiskey. "Hurry back," she said with a hand to my chest.

I held it there for a moment, then watched her walk away. I stood in the empty hallway for a few extra moments. Closing my eyes, I let the love I felt in that moment drain from my body. I let every good intention in my mind slip away as I refocused on what I had to do next.

I walked past Professor Wallace's door, not bothering to stop. I lied. I didn't hang back to speak to him. I had other plans.

I walked for several minutes. This part of the kingdom was empty. It was also cooler and darker. I hadn't been here in quite some time. Just one light illuminated the concrete stairs leading down. One could barely make out the steps, but with a manticore's vision, it was enough. Besides, hardly anyone came down here. I didn't plan to return for a very long time after tonight.

"Hunter," the guard addressed me as I walked into the damp hallway. Steel bars surrounded us and my eyes landed on my prey.

I turned to the guard, catching his eyes. He nodded once, handed me a key, and left me alone in the dungeons with Mathias.

I approached the steel bars, my fingers sliding across the cool metal.

"I knew you would come." He watched me, cracking his knuckles.

"I'm glad my reputation precedes me."

"You don't have what it takes to kill in cold blood," he said.

Naïve, little boy. I smiled at him.

"I don't plan to kill you, Mathias," I said. Then slipped the key into the lock. I took one last look down the hall before closing the door behind me. "But you will wish you were dead."

He swung first, but I ducked, punching him in the stomach. He reeled back but caught his balance.

"Come on, Mathias," I taunted, waving him toward me. "Don't make this easy."

He ran headfirst toward me, but I caught him under the shoulders and threw him to the dirty ground. I was done playing. I straddled his hips and pounded his face with my bare fists. He tried to shield himself but failed.

Punch after punch, blood dripped from his nose, ears, and eyes until he dropped his arms and I sat back on his legs. He spat a mouthful of blood by my knee and smiled, thinking I had done my worst. But I wasn't finished with him. Picturing him on top of Michaela, I lost my mind.

I pulled out my knife and held it to his groin. For the first time, terror flashed across his eyes.

"You fucking hurt her," I shouted, then pounded my chest. "My wife!" I roared in his face.

His eyes grew as large as my fists. His body shook, and the predator in me triumphed at his fear. Venom dripped from my fangs and I bit into his shoulder, tearing at his flesh.

He groaned but bit his lip, holding back his scream. He knew how much I craved the satisfaction of hearing his torment. I pressed the knife through the fabric of his pants and he whimpered.

He shook his head and tears fell from his eyes.

"You will never hurt anyone again," I said, my voice deeper than I'd ever heard it before.

He nodded in agreement.

"No, not because you're stuck in here," I said. "But because of this."

I sank my knife to the hilt, penetrating his limp flesh, and twisted.

His high-pitched scream finally satisfied my bloodlust.

***

I showered at the kingdom. I wanted to wash everything about Mathias Pedersen off of me and not bring any part of that into our home.

Michaela held Violet in her arms when I walked into our apartment. Violet was asleep, her smooth, rounded cheek on her mother's shoulder, as Michaela's hand circled her tiny back.

"Where were you?" she asked. Her voice was flat and hard.

I hung up my jacket, gathering the right words, racing circles in my head.

"I called the professor," she continued. "I needed to relay a message, but he said he hadn't seen you since the trial."

I rubbed my face and looked her straight in the eye.

"Your lying has to stop," she whispered, but her tone was threatening. "I mean it, Hunter."

I nodded. I hated hurting her and no matter the excuse; she was right. I had to stop.

She turned on her heels to leave the room, but then looked over her shoulder at me. "Did you hurt him?" she asked, her voice low, her eyes holding mine.

I wouldn't lie again. My voice shook, but I told her the truth. "Yes."

She held my gaze. I couldn't bring myself to apologize. Her eyes were hard and her lips straight.

"Good," she said.

Then she closed the bedroom door behind her.

Twenty-Nine

Michaela

I was angry at Hunter for three days. He had lied again. I knew this was an issue in our marriage that would take time to work through, *but dammit*, I couldn't believe he'd done it so soon. After a while, my anger waned. Despite his deceit, I was glad he'd hurt him.

Three days had passed since the trial, and I was finally feeling more like myself again. I awoke to Hunter's caress this morning. I knew he wanted to make love, but it felt rushed because I was late for work again. He ended up leaving for the office before I did.

Holding Violet in my arms, I pressed the elevator button for my grandmother's floor.

"Michaela, *bella*, you look exhausted," she said, taking Violet from my arms.

"I am," I admitted. "Is it okay if you and Violet stay at your place for the day? Hunter said some men were coming by our apartment to fix a few things and I didn't want the workers disturbing Violet's nap."

"Yes, of course. *Piccolina* will be comfortable here."

"Thanks, N*onna*." I kissed her cheek, then Violet's, and left for work.

The day proved to be a long one. I had to catch up on meetings with new clients and lessons for the academy. I missed my students the most.

Hunter called earlier, said he would drive me back home, and I was glad we'd have a few minutes alone before picking up Violet. When I climbed into the car, his eyes raked over me and I smiled. His heated glance always made me feel like the luckiest woman on earth.

"Hi," I said and leaned over to kiss him.

"Hi," he smiled and started the car.

"How was your day?" he asked.

"Good. Glad it's over and I get to come home to you and Violet."

He reached over and grabbed my hand. The intimacy warmed me. I admit I'd been cold the last few days since the trial.

Hunter drove straight to our apartment building, parked the car out front, and held my hand as we took the elevator to my grandmother's floor. Once the elevator doors closed, I grabbed his arm, dropped my head on his bicep, and sighed. He gathered me into his arms and rested his chin on top of my head. Closing my eyes, I inhaled his woodsy scent. It never failed to excite me.

"Are you tired?" he asked softly.

"No, just drained, but I'm feeling much better now," I teased.

He chuckled and smoothed his hand down my arm and around my shoulder until it rested on the small of my back. He pulled me closer to him, and I could feel his muscles tense. I raised my eyes and his amber ones stared back at me. He brought his head down and kissed my neck. My body melted in his arms.

Ding.

Ugh, elevators had the worst timing.

"Don't worry," he said with a smile. "I'll pick up where we just left off, later."

"You promise?" I teased.

"Yes, ma'am," he growled.

I knocked on my grandmother's door, and she quickly opened it. Her apartment differed greatly from ours. Where our kitchen and furniture were light, she preferred darker wood cabinets, black sofas, and purple and blue pillows. Violet lay on a red Persian carpet, tugging on the tassels.

"Oh, there you are," I said and dropped to the floor to pick her up. "Oh, mama missed you so much," I said and squeezed her chubby cheek next to mine.

"Ma-ma-ma-ma," she babbled.

"What! What did you say?" I asked, holding her back and watching her lips. She had never made that sound. "Did she say, mama?" I turned behind me. "Hunter, did you hear that?"

"Nope," he said and held back his grin as he bent down next to us. I smacked his arm.

"Oh, you have exceptional hearing. You heard it, don't lie."

"Fine, she may have used different consonants this time."

"No, she said mama," I argued. Turning back to Violet, "Didn't you, sweetheart?"

Violet's purple eyes stared back at mine, and she smiled. "Dadadada," she called out, and I frowned. "Well, she said it before."

Hunter laughed this time and put his arms around me. "I heard it, too. Don't worry," he quipped.

"Where's her bag?" I asked my grandmother while looking around her apartment. Usually, she kept the bag near the door when we came to pick up Violet.

"Violet is staying with Ramona one more night if that's all right with you," said Hunter, a grin spreading across his face.

"She is?" I asked my grandmother, but she didn't answer. She looked distracted, busy stirring a large pot in the kitchen.

"She is," said Hunter, cupping my cheek. "I need a night with you all to myself, especially after thinking I'd never see you again."

I kissed the top of Violet's head and whispered, "See you in the morning, baby girl."

"Are you two staying for dinner?" asked my grandmother, wiping her hands on her apron. The aroma of garlic, onions, and tomatoes wafted toward me and I swallowed it whole in a deep breath. I was a little tempted to have a quick bite first.

"Not tonight, Ramona. I've taken care of it," said Hunter, grabbing my hand. "Thanks again for watching Violet tonight."

"My pleasure," said Ramona. "I adore every moment I spend with my grandbaby. I feel as though I'm making up for so much lost time with my girls."

My grandmother had abandoned her daughters when they were adults. She didn't agree with the path my mother had taken and I nearly didn't forgive my grandmother for it. But forgiving her was one of the best things I'd ever done.

Hunter tugged on my arm lightly—his impatience was adorable. I couldn't help but hold back a laugh. "Goodnight, sweetie," I cooed to Violet.

"Oh, it's going to be one hell of good a night," Hunter whispered in my ear and suddenly I was the one racing to the front door.

"Bye, Nonna," I called out right before I ran down the hallway. Hunter caught up to me at the elevators and pinned me against the cold steel doors. A shiver ran down my back, but there was nothing but heat in front of me. His breath next to my ear raised goosebumps along my arms and God knows where else.

The elevator binged, and this time, instead of stopping, Hunter picked me up from the waist and carried me inside the elevator. I wrapped my legs around his hips and held on while he licked his way from my neck down to my collarbone, then lower still. My head fell back and a small moan slipped from my lips.

"I love it when you make those sounds," he growled.

In no time at all, the elevator doors pulled apart and Hunter carried me down the hallway toward our doorstep. His hand rummaged inside his coat pocket for the keys. It was taking him way too long, but I may have been distracting him with my tongue in his mouth.

Finally, he opened the door and carried me across the threshold. For a moment, I felt like a new bride again, instead of a tired parent.

Hunter kicked the door closed behind us. "Hungry?" he asked.

"Famished," I said and continued planting kisses along his neck.

"Good." He bent down and set me on my feet. A little disappointed he didn't carry me straight to the bedroom, I turned to walk that way myself. Only the scene before me halted my steps.

Strung patio lights twinkled throughout the living room. A picnic basket sat on top of a faux grass carpet. Beside the basket stood a telescope.

I raised my hands and covered my mouth. "Oh, my goodness," I said, my heart hammering in my chest. Then I turned to Hunter with tears in my eyes. "You've recreated our first date."

He pulled me closer to the faux grass. He had moved the furniture out of the way and so we walked over unhindered by couches and tables and sat down. "I'm glad you remembered," he said.

"Of course, I remembered. It was the best night of my life, right before it became one of the worst." I pulled his shirt collar into my fist. "You broke up with me a few hours later."

He placed his hand over mine. "That's why I wanted a do-over. I want tonight to end differently. The way I imagined it would end in my mind." He kissed my lips softly. "That night, all I wanted to do was lay you down on this carpet and make love to you."

My breath caught in my throat. His words still had that effect on me. All I could do was nod and my fingers fumbled to release the top button on my white fitted blouse. He pulled his shirt from his body, one shoulder at a time, exposing his chiseled stomach. Entranced, I ran my fingers across the ridges of his abdomen and his muscles jumped in response. He finished unbuttoning my blouse while I ran my hands across his familiar chest. Every muscle, every sinew, burned itself into my mind. "You're not going to stop and ask me to go shopping, are you?"

"No fucking way," he growled and pulled my face closer, cupping the back of my head. He kissed me hard and thoroughly. His mouth was relentless and his fervor only excited me more. My hands reached for the button on his pants and he did the same with mine. He pulled away, and I stood there, bare to his gaze. The heat from his eyes warmed me, and I bent down to my knees.

He joined me on the carpet and pulled me down. The grass tickled my back and the unusual sensation made me sensitive everywhere. Hunter reached over me to open the picnic basket. He pulled out a container of chocolate-covered strawberries and brought a bright red one to my lips. I opened my mouth and took a bite. The sweet flavor of the fruit with the dark chocolate exploded on my tongue. I closed my eyes to savor the taste.

When I opened them, Hunter was watching me, the intensity in his eyes making my stomach dip. I raised my arm to grab a strawberry and feed him, but he shook his head. "I have other plans," he said and continued to kiss his way along every curve of my body.

I suddenly became self-conscious of the areas that had changed since Violet was born—they were softer, heavier. With both hands on either of his cheeks, I guided him away from those parts. He looked up, but I avoided his gaze. I was too embarrassed to meet his eyes. "I love every inch of your body. Don't push me away."

"But it's not the same as it used to be," I said, despising the words but hating it more that I didn't regret them.

"Don't you see it? I'm more attracted to you today than I was a year ago. Every day I am with you, my attraction—God help me—intensifies. I just want to be with you, Michaela. Let me love you," he whispered.

I let his face slip through my fingers and didn't stop him this time. I freed my mind to not think of my body and instead to just feel. Feel his love pouring out of his lips. Feel his strength moving within his muscles. But mostly, letting myself feel loved and desired.

To feel worthy of unconditional love—regardless that my body had changed. Tears ran down my eyes, the emotion of letting go rushed through me. The tension released, and I let out a breath of satisfaction. "I love you," I whispered. He moaned, and I smiled.

"We're just getting started," he said.

"This is definitely better than our first date," I laughed.

Thirty

Hunter

I didn't have the heart to wake Michaela. Her slumbering body lay peacefully in the faux grass, her curls intertwined with the green blades. We never made it to the bedroom last night, the memory made me grin.

Exhausted, we both fell asleep on the floor. I'd mustered just enough energy to pull a blanket over us before I blacked out. Now in the light of day, I let her rest and stepped into the bathroom to shower, then pick up Violet.

Ramona had Violet's bag ready at the door, and the gurgling little cherub was already dressed and scampering around. She was on the same Persian carpet where we had left her last night.

"I think she's teething," said Ramona, walking over to Violet to wipe the drool from her lips. She tried to take the beads away from her mouth, but Violet growled and bit down on Ramona's finger.

"Ouch!" said Ramona, shaking the sore finger. "No, *piccolina*, you cannot bite, little one!" She waved a pointed finger at the baby. Violet frowned but otherwise she seemed unphased by the scolding.

"Let me see your finger, Ramona," I said, walking across the carpet.

Ramona stuck out her ring finger, and I pulled it closer to take a look. It was red and still bleeding. The puncture was deep. I picked up Violet and ran my finger along her gums. She didn't have teeth yet, but I felt divots in certain spots. A thought crossed my mind.

I put Violet back down on the ground but kept my finger on her gums. She sucked playfully and even pressed down now and then. When I pulled her beads away with my free hand, the little sprite noticed and got angry. And that's when I felt them. Her incisors poked out from underneath her gums and punctured my skin. *Damn.*

"Did she bite you, too?" asked Ramona.

"She did," I said, looking up from the carpet at the older woman. Her eyes, so much like Michaela's and now Violet's, stared back at me. "Looks like she got something from me after all."

"Do you think she's venomous?" asked Ramona.

"I do not know for certain. But I think we should treat her like she is. I wouldn't let Nicholas or any other human hold her until she can control her instincts better."

Ramona nodded. My head spun. *What did this mean?* There was no other child in the world like Violet and that wasn't just a father talking. It was the truth. I had to discuss this with Michaela and decide what we needed to do to protect our little girl and those around her. With manticores, we simply kept them home until they were old enough to control their instincts. Usually, that was around the age of three or four. I wasn't sure if Violet was venomous or if she even had the instincts of a predator. Only time would tell us for certain.

"Thanks, Ramona," I said, lifting Violet back into my arms. "I'm going to take this little one back home with me. I appreciate everything you've done for us."

"You're welcome, Hunter." Then to Violet, "I'll see you later, *piccolina.*" Violet happily chomped on her beads and kicked her legs.

She babbled throughout the entire elevator ride up to our penthouse suite and even after I opened the door to our apartment. Michaela wasn't in the living room; she wasn't anywhere that I could see her, in fact. "Michaela?" I called out.

She poked her head from our bedroom door. "Hey, Hunter. Oh,

there's my baby girl." She wore a white robe and her hair was wet. "Give me a second to get dressed and I'll be right out."

I held Violet against my chest as I paced the apartment. She weighed nothing in my arms, but my mind was a different story. A few minutes later, Michaela joined us. She wore casual grey pants and a white sweater. She'd braided her hair in the brief time she was in the bathroom.

"Here, let me hold her," she said, picking Violet up from my arms.

"Michaela, we need to talk," I said, trying to find the right words to explain my suspicions.

"Sure," she said, but she wasn't looking at me. She was fussing with Violet's clothes, straightening out her dress.

"Oh, before I forget, Leo called," she said.

"He called here? Why didn't he call my cell phone?"

"He tried, but the ringer was off, he had said."

I pulled out my phone and noticed I'd missed two calls from Leo. I put my phone on silent last night, not wanting to be disturbed while on my 'date' with Michaela, and forgot to put the ringer back on this morning. I was about to turn my phone off when Leo's name flashed across my screen.

"What did you want to talk about?" Michaela asked.

"Ah, just give me a minute to see what he wants," I said, holding up a finger, then answered the call. "Leo, hey, I had my phone on silent."

"I'm glad I caught you," he said. "Do you have a minute to meet me this morning? It's important."

"Can we meet in about an hour?" I wanted to speak to Michaela first.

"An hour could be too late. I was hoping to meet with you sooner but I couldn't get a hold of you."

I gave in. "All right, where should we meet?"

"At the coffee place by your apartment," he confirmed.

"When?"

"I'm already here."

I groaned inwardly but then said, "I'll be down in a moment."

Michaela looked up when I ended the call. "Sounds important," she said.

"Yes, it does," I agreed.

"Can it wait, whatever you wanted to talk about?"

"Yes, looks like it will have to." I leaned down and kissed her, then Violet. "I'll be back soon." She smiled and waved Violet's little hand at me. "Say bye, Violet."

"Babababa," Violet squealed. Michaela squeezed her closer. "Ah, you're going to be talking in no time."

***

I found Leo staring at his phone when I arrived at the coffee-house. He sat with one leg crossed over the other, leaning back in his chair, wearing a full grey suit and a striped white and grey tie. He spotted me as soon as I walked in.

"Hunter, thank you for coming," he said.

"It didn't sound like I had much of a choice," I countered.

He cleared his throat. "Yes, well, I wanted to be polite but if we are doing away with all civilities, let me get right into it."

I waved my hand, motioning him to proceed.

"We have a problem," he began.

I groaned. I had just returned from being kidnapped, rescued by my wife, who had to fight for her life because of my aunt, and now we have a problem again. "Are you sure we have a problem?" I tilted my head, hoping my hunch was correct.

"It's Scarlet," he said.

"Ah, so I'm right. It sounds like *you* have a problem."

"Can I get you something?" A server asked, holding a pot of coffee. I turned over the mug in front of me. "Just a black coffee is good."

After she poured my coffee, she smiled at me and left. I crossed my arms across my chest and leaned back in my chair. Leo fidgeted in his seat the entire time the server was near, biting his tongue, I was certain. When she left, he leaned forward.

"No, it's still *we*," he hissed at me.

"Fine, why do we have a problem with Scarlet?" I drawled, enjoying the way the usual calm Leo was now worked up over a girl.

"Well, for starters..." he glanced up and out the window. Something had caught his attention. He swore softly, "Oh, bloody hell."

I turned in my seat and watched the familiar red hair and long legs of none other than Scarlet Reynolds approach us. I had first seen Scarlet in a dark New York alleyway. She was in the grips of another rogue manticore, Jenkins. I got there in time that night and Scarlet escaped unharmed. Weeks later, unfortunately, Jenkins returned to her apartment to finish what he had started. But Leo and I were there and Scarlet ended up stabbing Jenkins in the leg before I killed him. Scarlet and Leo had made a connection. I felt it in the room that night and they confirmed it when he brought her to our engagement dinner. But when Scarlet had not come to the wedding, I'd figured Leo made the right decision and let her go. Obviously, there was more to this story.

"Were you not expecting her?" I asked.

"No," he ground out. "I've been avoiding her until I spoke to you. She must have followed me or figured I'd be close to your apartment." He rubbed the back of his neck, then ran his fingers through his hair.

"This woman really has you all tangled up inside," I said. "You know you can't be with her."

"I know that," he snapped. "This isn't about her and me. This is about all manticores. That's why I needed to speak to you. Hunter—"

Leo wasn't able to finish the rest because Scarlet had walked into the coffeehouse and stood behind Leo. She had her hands on her hips and a frown on her face.

"Good morning, Scarlet. A pleasure to see you," I said.

Her lips curved into a slight smile only to fall back down when she looked at Leo. "It's good to see you, too, Hunter," she said, still looking down at Leo.

He cleared his throat. "Why Scarlet," he said, standing up. "What a pleasant surprise to see you here. Fancy that. It's not like you were following me or something."

"Yes, I was following you, as a matter of fact," she admitted. "You managed to evade me several times, but not today."

"Yes, I thought you were at work," Leo mumbled under his breath, but I heard him. Both Leo and I stood to offer Scarlet our chair, but Leo waved me down. "Please take my seat," he said with a forced smile and turned to pull up an unoccupied chair from another table.

"Why have you been following Leo?" I asked when she sat in front of me.

"Because she has good taste," Leo quipped beside me, but Scarlet shot him a glare.

"No, because he hasn't gotten back to me," she said, placing her clasped hands on the table. "I plan to run a story about manticores for the New York Gazette and I want Leo to go on record."

I tilted my head and narrowed my eyes, focusing on Scarlet's features. Her eyes gripped mine and her lips did not twitch as though she held back a smile. "You're not kidding?" I asked.

"No," she said, still holding my gaze.

I turned to Leo. "That's what I needed to talk to you about," he said, crossing his arms and blowing out a breath.

"Well, I wasn't expecting that. You caught me off guard," I

replied, honestly. Then a million questions raced through my mind, but the only word that came out was, "Why?"

Leo leaned forward, "Scarlet, if this is about how things ended between us—"

"This isn't about you, Leo, or me, for that matter," she said. "This is about protecting other people. We have a right to know that manticores exist and what they are capable of, so we can protect ourselves."

"Scarlet, even if you knew that manticores existed before Jenkins grabbed you in the alleyway, you wouldn't have been able to stop him. We are faster, stronger, and always have a weapon on us." I tapped on my fingernails, but she didn't need the reminder.

"That's not the point, Hunter," she argued. "We have a right to know what we're dealing with."

I shook my head. "And I took an oath to protect the members of my kingdom. If you publish that story, it will cause an uproar. Hundreds, maybe more, will begin hunting for manticores and many will think they've found one when they really haven't. It will turn into those horrible witch trials. Do you really want what happened in Salem on your hands?"

"This is a different time. People are not like that anymore," said Scarlet, but her eyes twitched.

I raised my eyebrow. "Do you really believe that? Are you willing to risk people's lives in case you're wrong?"

"We cannot go on as though manticores do not exist!" she shouted. Fortunately, no one turned around.

"Yes, we can and we must," I told her. "We've done it for thousands of years and will do it for thousands of years after today. It is the only way, Scarlet."

"But Michaela accepted it. I accept it. Others will too."

"I'm not willing to risk it," I said and stood up from the table. "If that's what you came to say, then I think we're done here. I will not give Leo permission for this interview." I leaned down and let my chest rumble. "And I strongly suggest, Scarlet, that you forget all about it."

A visible shiver ran through Scarlet. She closed her eyes, and I could smell her fear. I hated using my predator instincts on her, but she needed to realize her story would not happen. With no corroborating witnesses, she had nothing to stand on.

I buttoned my jacket and was about to walk away when her next words stopped me. "What about Violet?"

My daughter's name froze me in place. I inhaled a calming breath, as I truly did not want to hurt Scarlet. She'd been through enough. "What about her?" I asked, my tone negating the tension I felt inside.

"Is she a manticore? Or is she human? How will she navigate this new world?"

I released the breath I was holding. "I appreciate your concern, Scarlet. But Michaela and I have it under control."

Before I left, I turned to Leo in a whisper I knew only he could hear. "Take care of this. She cannot write anything about manticores."

He nodded, but he focused his eyes on Scarlet, who was staring at the both of us, trying to listen with no doubt.

"Will do," he said. And I left him to deal with Scarlet. I did not envy him. But I had another conversation I needed to deal with back in my apartment. Violet's name reminded me that I needed to speak to Michaela about what happened in Ramona's apartment.

When I returned home, I found Michaela in the study. She was typing away on her laptop, a video monitor next to her. I picked up the monitor and smiled when I saw Violet sprawled out in her crib. Roxy, Michaela's old teddy bear, beside her. "What are you working on?" I asked.

"Oh, just an upcoming media tour. I have one more appointment to book, then I'm done." She was staring at her screen but then turned to look at me. "How did everything go with Leo?"

"Well, he was right, we do have a problem," I said, and she took off her blue-light glasses and turned in her chair to face me.

"What happened?" she asked.

"I'll catch you up in a minute. First, I need to tell you something that happened in Ramona's apartment when I picked up Violet." Michaela's eyes flickered to the monitor, instinctively checking on our daughter.

"Okay. What happened?"

"Violet bit down on Ramona's finger," I said.

Michaela laughed. "The little rascal. She's teething, so she will chomp her gums down on anything in front of her."

"She punctured her skin. Ramona was bleeding."

Her smile disappeared. "What are you talking about? She doesn't have any teeth yet."

I ran my fingers through my hair and looked up at the ceiling. "She doesn't have any we can see yet. But I felt them. When she got angry, her incisors lengthened and briefly came through her gums.

"Oh my God," she said, putting a hand to her mouth. "Is my grandmother okay?"

"Yes, she's fine, of course. Her body and blood can handle a manticore's venom. But she's not the one I'm worried about."

Michaela shook her head. "You're right. I am clueless about this stuff, Hunter. What do you do with baby manticores?"

I shifted my weight, knowing she would not be happy to hear this. "Well, we keep them away from humans until they can control their instincts."

"Keep her away? For how long?"

"Three or four years," I explained.

"Three or four years? But she's supposed to start daycare soon, then preschool. We can't keep her isolated for that long. It's not healthy."

"I know. But we won't be able to assimilate her with other human children until we know for sure she can control herself."

"So where do we take her in the meantime?" she asked, her eyes glancing at the monitor.

"To our kingdom. We will have to reach out to other manticore families with children her age and do the best we can with what we have. It won't be for a very long time, I promise." I reached out and gently ran my finger across her cheek. She looked up at me, still sitting in her chair, "But if she isn't fully a manticore, they may not accept her."

"They will. I will demand it."

"That's not how it works," she said with a sad smile.

"We will find a way to raise her in this uncharted path. I swear it."

Her smile this time was genuine. She stood and put her arms around me. "We will find a way, Hunter." She stood on her tiptoes and kissed me. The feel of her lips on mine always stoked the fire that continuously burned for her. Too tired to fight it, I fueled the fire instead. I bent and kissed her, stoking the fire with my tongue. She let out a surprised little gasp.

"You're going to have to book that last appointment later," I said. "You've got a very important meeting with me right now."

She threw her head back and laughed. I squeezed her tighter in my arms.

Thirty-One

Michaela

I rubbed the chrome finish with a microfiber cloth, making it gleam.

"I think that's it," I said to my best friend Dev, picking up my phone. His soft brown eyes stared back at me. He had cut his hair shorter than the last time I'd seen him in Toronto.

"Hunter is definitely going to be surprised," said Dev, chuckling.

I wiped a bead of sweat from my forehead with the back of my hand. "I hope he won't be angry with the new install."

"Angry? Girl, you're going to have to tie him up."

I raised my eyebrow. "That's not a bad idea." Then we both laughed.

"How's English Breakfast Tea?" I asked when I caught my breath.

"Michaela, you didn't forget his name, did you?" I couldn't be sure from this angle, but I pictured Dev's hand flying onto his hip.

I laughed again. It was so easy to do with Dev. "Of course not. I know his name is Rudra."

"Well, he's good. We're good. I think things are getting pretty serious. He asked me to a family dinner."

"That's great news, Dev. I know the perfect gift you can bring."

"If you say tea, I'm never speaking to you again," he deadpans.

I fall onto the bed, holding my middle from my fit of laughter. "All right, I won't." Glancing at the time, my stomach flipped, only this time for a different reason. "I better go shower. Hunter will be home soon and I don't want to be a hot mess."

"Who knows, that may help your cause."

"Thanks for the advice. I'll let you know how it goes."

"You better!" he said and puckered his lips to blow me a kiss.

"Love you, too," I said and blew him a kiss back.

After ending the call, I quickly showered and dressed in the new outfit I'd purchased only this morning. I bought a few other pieces, tired of feeling uncomfortable in my old clothes and ready to rock my new body.

I thought I'd have more time to walk around in these heels to break them in, but the install took all day with Dev walking me through it on the phone. I smoothed down my skirt and pushed up my bra when the front door opened.

"Michaela, I'm home," Hunter called.

"I'm just in the bedroom getting changed."

I glanced at the blue wrap dress I'd worn for the graduation ceremony hanging in my closet. I contemplated changing into it, getting cold feet all of a sudden.

You can do this, Michaela.

"Where's Violet?" Hunter said from the living room.

"She's with my grandmother," I shouted. Then, hearing his footsteps nearby, I added, "Don't come in yet."

I took one last look at myself in the full-length mirror and inhaled deeply. *Here goes nothing.*

I pressed play on my phone, and a jazzy saxophone crooned from my Bluetooth speakers. The footsteps halted. Then a knock sounded on the bedroom door.

"Come in," I said, my voice cracking. I cleared my throat, tossed my hair and shoulders back, and placed a hand on my hip.

Hunter took a tentative step into the room, his eyes meeting my new installation first. "What is—"

Then his eyes found me, and he was speechless.

I grinned, and my confidence grew by the second. "Do you like it?" I asked, my voice low, as I raked a nail straight down my chest, over the black lace bra, then resting on the short leather skirt that barely covered my cheeks. The thong I wore didn't help either.

Hunter nodded once, then swallowed. His eyes raked over my body, and my skin tingled as though he had touched me. I swayed my hips along to the music, slowly, seductively. I closed my eyes, losing myself in the movements.

When he stepped closer, I raised the palm of my hand. "No touching the dancers," I said. He groaned but didn't say a word. He sat down on the plush armchair in our bedroom and watched me as I walked over to the pole that took all day to install.

I wrapped my leg and hand around the pole and swung around once. My eyes trained on Hunter as I watched him squeeze the chair's armrest. I pressed my back up against the pole and slid down low, my knees opening to him. His eyes locked on my thong as he wet his lips. I closed my thighs shut, and he growled.

Raising my arm above my head, I pulled myself up and turned my back to him. Bending forward, I dropped and touched the floor. His fingers were on my inner thigh in a second. I turned my head over my shoulder to admonish him and the look in his eyes stole my breath. His mouth opened slightly, his eyes burning into mine, and his nostrils flared.

"I'm not finished with my dance," I said.

"I can't take another minute of just watching you," he said, his voice hoarse. "I'm glad my eyes are the only ones on you this time."

I pushed him back onto the chair, kicked off my heels, and rested my bare foot on his thigh. He circled my ankle with his fingers and worked his way up. When he reached behind my knee, my leg wobbled. "I love that I know all your spots."

Then he dropped his head to kiss my inner thigh.

"I think it's time you sat back and enjoyed my performance," he murmured.

I dropped my head back. "That sounds really good."

He lifted me over his shoulder, as he'd done in Norway, and carried me toward the bed.

Grinning, I smacked him on the back. "You know, you don't have to do that."

He turned his head to look at me. "I thought we were recreating a moment?"

A thought popped into my head. "I was going to remove the pole tomorrow, but I might keep it a little longer," I told him, looking over my shoulder.

He dropped me onto the bed. "That thing is never coming down," he murmured and removed his tie.

"What are we going to tell Violet?" I chuckled.

"That her daddy's a fireman."

I laughed, throwing my head back onto the pillow, and Hunter's lips curled into a smile at my neck.

"I love you so much," he said, rising onto his elbow.

He ran a finger down my cheek. "I love your laugh." Moving his finger to my temple, he continued. "I love your eyes and your eyebrows."

When I arched those eyebrows in reply, he grinned. "Yes, especially when you do that." He smoothed the crease between them with his fingertip.

I grabbed his finger and brought it to my heart. "I love you, too. I'm glad we're both stubborn and found a way."

He smiled.

We never gave up. Not when things got hard, not when ruthless manticores demanded us to. We fought to protect each other, no matter the consequences.

Hunter cupped my face between his hands. "I will do whatever it takes to protect you and Violet, I promise."

"I know," I whispered, leaning forward. He caught my lower lip between his teeth and pulled. This time, a playful grin danced on his face.

We had gone through so much, lived through the worst of my nightmares, and still loved as passionately as new lovers do. It was not because our love hadn't changed but because it had changed along with us.

Neither creed nor circumstances could keep us apart. The path for us hadn't been easy. But nothing in life worth fighting for ever was.

***

Thank you for joining me on this journey!

If you enjoyed this book, please consider leaving a review or rating. It helps indie authors tremendously.

Have you read the prequel, **VIOLET SKY First Love**? How about the Contemporary Romance **Push & Pull**? If not, check them out today! To download them for free, visit my website, www.evemarian.com.

Acknowledgement

This book was written thanks to my cousin Gilda. When I was ready to move on and write a spin-off, she told me Michaela and Hunter needed one more story. She was right. I needed to explore what happens after the happily ever after, and the answer was—life.

To my husband, Antonio, and children Patricia and Gabriel, thank you for your unwavering support.

To my critique partner Kandie, who stuck by me and helped me make this story so much better. I still want to write about Huldra one day, but perhaps she deserves her own story.

To my writing group, Anuja, Nita, Nadja, and Jayme, thank you for listening and offering advice whenever I needed it.

To the TikTok community, your generous spirit and enthusiasm picked me up whenever I felt down. Your support made all the difference on those days when I didn't know what to write. Thank you for making this new author feel welcomed.

To anyone who has purchased a copy of the first two books, I don't know how to thank you enough for making my dreams come true. My heart belongs to you.

About The Author

Eve Marian is a former journalist and public relations executive. She lives in a suburb of Toronto with her husband, two children, and clever cat named Chase.

To receive the latest information on new releases, giveaways, promotions, and more, sign up for her newsletter at www.evemarian.com.

www.ingramcontent.com/pod-product-compliance
Lightning Source LLC
Chambersburg PA
CBHW030338310726
48979CB00001B/89
9781778026201